THE CAPTAIN
AND
MISS WINTER
by Sally Britton

Titles by Sally Britton:

The Branches of Love Series

Martha's Patience, a novella
#1 *The Social Tutor*
#2 *The Gentleman Physician*
#3 *His Bluestocking Bride*
#4 *The Earl and His Lady*
#5 *Miss Devon's Choice*
#6 *Courting the Vicar's Daughter* (Spring 2019)

The Captain and Miss Winter

Other Titles in the Forever After Series:

Beauty and the Baron, by Joanna Barker
The Steadfast Heart, by Arlem Hawks

The Captain and Miss Winter

Sally Britton

The Captain and Miss Winter © 2019 by Sally Britton. All Rights Reserved.

All rights reserved. No part of this book may be reproduced in any form or by any electronic or mechanical means, including information storage and retrieval systems, without permission in writing from the author. The only exception is by a reviewer, who may quote short excerpts in a review.

Cover design: Blue Water Books

This book is a work of fiction. Names, characters, places, and incidents either are products of the author's imagination or are used fictitiously. Any resemblance to actual persons, living or dead, events, or locales is entirely coincidental.

Sally Britton
www.authorsallybritton.com

First Printing: February 2019

To my husband, forever and always.

And to anyone in search of happily ever after.

One evening, as they were thus sitting comfortably together, someone knocked at the door as if he wished to be let in. The mother said: 'Quick, Rose-red, open the door, it must be a traveler who is seeking shelter.' Rose-red went and pushed back the bolt, thinking that it was a poor man, but it was not; it was a bear that stretched his broad, black head within the door.

—The Brothers Grimm

(*Grimms' Fairy Tales*, trans. by Edgar Taylor and Marian Edwardes)

Chapter One

FEBRUARY 1816

Once upon a time, Caspar Graysmark had thought a career in the military would be precisely everything he wanted. That was before he actually joined the British army, before he'd marched through the war-torn countries of Europe, living in the dirt and subsisting on rations of moldy bread and wilted cabbages.

Freezing rain came down in sheets, and he could see nothing before or behind him in the bare-branched forest. The night remained black and cold. He was lost, somewhere near the Franco-Spanish border, in the mountains east of Larrau, a village small enough it shouldn't even be on the map. A village he only knew to look for because he had been through it once before, leading a small company of men on a secret assignment.

And I'm just as lost now as I was then

He'd supposed that going to battle would be something he'd take to naturally, after all his years of playing soldier about his father's estate. But marching up and down the garden walk with his brothers was nothing like firing into a line of living, breathing men.

After Napoleon's surrender, Caspar had intended to go home to England and never leave its shores again. Except, as he explained in a letter to his mother, he had to perform one last task. One last deed that weighed upon him. His honor demanded he see it through.

Caspar shuddered and pulled his heavy fur coat closer about himself, then dismounted to lead his horse, Fortinbras. Perhaps on foot he would do a better job of navigating.

Ice crystals crunched beneath his feet, and the sleet turned to snow. If he didn't find shelter in short order, Caspar had little hope of him and his horse surviving until the next morning.

A flicker in the distance, between the dark trees, caught his weary gaze.

"Light," he whispered aloud. His horse snorted. "There's a light." He almost chuckled. Talking to his horse the past few days had become his only opportunity to hear his own voice in the wilds of hill and forest. He led the animal forward, his progress as slow as before but now more hopeful.

Down the other side of a hill he went, narrowly avoiding tree branches, his eyes fixed ahead on a small square of glowing orange.

He stepped out of the trees into a flat, clear space of land, yards away from the welcoming light. It had to be a window. It *had* to be a window. His mind wouldn't play such tricks on him.

His eyes took in more as he drew closer. It was a small stone house, a cottage. He kept moving, all the way to the window, his teeth chattering and bits of ice frozen to his beard and eyebrows.

Caspar didn't look through the window, only made for the door.

He knocked with the hand not holding his horse, then waited. Good breeding alone kept him from simply rushing inside to the source of warmth and brightness.

Scarlett's head jerked up from where it had rested on her sister's shoulder. Blanche sat upright, sucking in a sharp breath.

"Someone knocked," Blanche whispered, her wide eyes on the door. The orange tabby in her lap jumped down to hide beneath the bench.

"Who would be out in weather like this?" their grandmother asked, lowering her knitting needles. Her white eyebrows drew together. She met Scarlett's eyes. "Answer it, child."

Blanche remained where she sat, cautious and unwilling to act hastily, as always, and grandmother's old bones would ache too much if she moved far from the fire. It fell to Scarlett as the elder sister, as it usually did, to undertake a difficult task.

She stood, dropping her half of the blanket back onto the old bench. Adjusting her tattered shawl about her shoulders, she went across the room to the door.

She ought to ask who stood on the other side, given that the only thing protecting her from the elements, beasts, and less-than-savory men was the very door knocked upon. But truly, it wasn't the sturdiest of doors. If it was pushed hard enough, the bolt wouldn't even hold.

Scarlett tilted her chin upward and slid the bolt open, then swung the door open with all the confidence she could muster. Cold night air rushed inside, slipping around her feet to find the corners of their tiny cottage, like cats coming in from the weather. Scarlett hardly noticed, once she saw his eyes.

A giant of a man stood at their threshold, his striking blue eyes the only light thing about him. He was robed in dark furs, his face covered in a short beard, a hat low upon his brow. He was a head taller than she and at least twice as wide in his shoulders. She should've been frightened of him, and would've been, if not for those eyes.

He spoke in broken French, his voice deep and rumbling. "*S'il vous plaît. J'ai besoin d'un abri.*"

Her grandmother called to her in English. "Who is it, my flower?"

"A man," Scarlett answered, her voice only a whisper. She cleared her throat and raised her voice, though her eyes never left his face. "A man, asking for shelter."

"If he means us no harm, you had better let him inside."

Scarlett looked from his piercing gaze down to his stout boots and back up.

The man shook his head, his expression turning confused. "You speak English?" When was the last time she'd heard a man's voice speak her native tongue? Not since her father's death.

"We do." She stood on her toes to peer over his shoulder, seeing only a horse behind him. "If you wish for shelter here, you must give me your word you mean us no harm."

He nodded quickly. "On my honor, I wish no one in this house ill will, and more, I will do whatever is in my power to repay your kindness."

His manner of speech was cultured, and his tone low enough to make her feel its charm all the way through her bones. She shivered, and not from the cool air filling the space between them. "Very well. There is a shed against the cottage, just there." She pointed to the left of the door. "It's big enough for your horse. Put him there and then come back. We will give you shelter."

The man, despite his shivering, actually bowed to her. She could not remember the last time she'd been shown such courtesy. She closed the door, then rushed back the seven steps to the hearth, a blush warming her cheeks.

Their cottage only held two rooms; their sleeping chamber and the room they sat in made up the whole of the cottage. They had carpets that were not more than woven rags, a table with broken and mismatched chairs, and the bench she and her sister had covered with an old quilt and stuffed straw cushions. It was clean and tidy, but the floor was hard-packed earth, and all cooking was done over the same fire that kept them warm.

"He's coming in after he takes care of his horse," she announced to her sister and grandmother, as though they hadn't heard every word of the exchange between herself and the stranger. "What can we give him?"

Blanche rose and went to their hutch near the table, which acted as their pantry and larder both. She opened the cabinet and took out a wrapped loaf of bread and a jar of boiled chicken. "He can begin with bread, and we will add the chicken to our stew."

"A wise idea," their grandmother said. The stew pot hung on a hook they could swing in and out of the fire. "We'll warm his insides as best we can. What a night to be out wandering in the woods!"

Scarlett went back to the door, listening for the stranger's return and watching her sister hurry to add chicken to the cooling pot, which had only contained carrots, cabbage, and a smattering of spices before.

She didn't question helping the stranger. Not on a night like this. Not after looking into his eyes.

Even if he was a thief, they had little enough to steal. Their clothes were worn thin, their precious things had long since been sold or bartered away; all they truly had left was each other.

She heard the crunch of footsteps outside the door and opened it, standing aside to allow the large man entry. Though she knew their cottage to be small, it had never felt as tiny as it did when he stepped inside. The man filled the very air they breathed.

Scarlett closed and bolted the door behind him.

"Thank you," he said, the words clipped from between his chattering teeth. "You have saved me."

Scarlett bit her bottom lip, looking to her grandmother for guidance.

"Come in, sir. Come and share our fire. Scarlett, take his coat," Grandmother instructed, not moving from her place by the hearth. Blanche stood behind Grandmother, her fingers gripping the back of their grandmother's chair.

The man bowed to them, then started to slip his arms free of the great fur coat on his back. Scarlett hurried to help him, taking the shoulders of the garment in her hands, catching it before it hit the floor. The fur was soaked through, nearly frozen, and weighed more than Scarlett expected. Barely keeping hold of it, she went to the table and laid the coat flat upon it. The frost glittered as it melted.

Her eyes went to the man, his back to her. He knelt in front of the fire, holding his hands out to the flame. His whole body still trembled from the cold.

Scarlett looked to Blanche, who met her eyes.

"Quilts," Scarlett said. Her sister nodded and disappeared into their bedroom.

"Sir," Scarlett said, coming near him. "Please, sit, let us take off your boots."

He didn't move to the bench, but sat down on the rug, not moving from the fire even an inch. He stretched his legs out before him, but before he could reach for his boots, Scarlett gripped the heel of one in her hands. She pulled, tugged, and got the large footwear off. She set it by the hearth and began work on the other.

His breeches were long and appeared to be well made. Not the apparel of a trapper or peasant. The man stripped off his gloves, not protesting her help.

Blanche returned, two quilts in her arms.

"Take off the rest of your wet things, young man," Grandmother said, her voice authoritative. "Then we can get you warm."

Young man? Scarlett's eyes raised from the boot in her hands up to his face. His bright blue eyes met hers. How could Grandmother tell? The dark brown beard he wore concealed most of his features.

"Yes, madam," he said, his deep voice rumbling through the small room. It was a pleasant voice, a soothing one.

He took off his hat, then the second coat he wore, and even his socks, all while sitting on their rug before the fire. While it should've been the most inelegant thing Scarlett had ever seen a man do, she found herself examining his broad shoulders, his strong fingers. He met her eyes after he draped his socks across the stones near the fire, and she realized she had been staring, holding his boot, kneeling not a foot away from him the whole time.

Scarlett's cheeks warmed. She moved backward, dropping the boot on the floor, and stood.

Blanche came forward with the quilts, her steps slow and eyes wary, bending to hand them both to the stranger.

The man thanked her, his voice quieter. He wrapped one quilt around his shoulders and laid the other over his lap, bundling himself up. His body had stopped quaking, his teeth no longer clacked together, and he looked about with some curiosity.

"Tell me," he said, looking from Scarlett to Grandmother. "How did three Englishwomen come to live in the middle of a French forest?"

Chapter Two

The women's silent exchange of glances and narrowing of eyes would've been amusing if Caspar wasn't so exhausted. Or so hungry. The smell of herbs warming in the pot nearly drove him to distraction as he tried to determine how many hours had passed since his breakfast of stale bread and cheese.

The dark-haired woman who opened the door to him was the one who finally answered his question. "My father was English. After my mother died, he brought my grandmother, my sister, and me to France. The war did to us what it did to many. I think the best English word to describe our circumstances is that we are *displaced*." The wary expression in her deep brown eyes, and the way the firelight and shadows danced upon her features, gave her an air of mystery.

Caspar nodded as if he understood, though she'd not satisfied his curiosity in the least, and said no more. It would be best not to pry, especially given that he would be frozen outside had they not opened their door to him.

"Are you hungry?" the elderly woman asked.

Caspar forced himself to show some restraint, attempting to act like a civilized man instead of a starving one. "I would not want to trouble you."

"He is starving," the talkative young woman said, one corner of her pretty mouth tilting upward in a smile he found more charming than her cautious gaze.

Recollecting his manners, Caspar realized he'd neglected the most basic requirement of a well-behaved gentleman. A proper introduction.

Pushing himself slowly to his feet, Caspar bowed to the old woman in the chair. "I beg your forgiveness, madam. I am Captain Graysmark, of the British army."

"And I am Mrs. Michaelson. My granddaughters are Miss Scarlett and Miss Blanche Winter." She gestured first to the woman with the captivating smile and then to the other, with gold hair. "Scarlett, please help the captain with his meal."

The young woman rose from her place on the floor with as much grace as any society miss he'd ever met, then went to the cupboard near the table. She came back to the fire, used a hook to remove the lid from the pot, then a ladle to fill a bowl with stew. Caspar's mouth watered and his insides clenched with hunger, and then a low sound, like a growl, escaped from his stomach.

The women all froze.

"Forgive me—" He broke off when he saw laughter in Miss Winter's eyes.

"Are you certain you are a man and not a bear, Captain? With your fur coat and sounds such as that, it is difficult to tell." Miss Winter spoke with one raised eyebrow.

Caspar looked at his coat laid out to dry, then raised a hand to touch the scruff of his beard. "I am afraid to say I can understand your confusion, Miss Winter." If he revealed his position as a man of consequence, an earl with estates and wealth, they likely would not believe him.

An amused quirk of her mouth was all the response he received before she handed him his bowl and a wooden spoon. "Eat, Captain. We already had our dinner and we do not stand upon ceremony here."

The grandmother clucked her tongue and picked up her knitting, and the other young woman stiffly took her seat on the bench. He swallowed his pride, ignored his good breeding, and ate as speedily as the hot food allowed. Though he had dined at many finer tables in his life, upon fine delicacies, the stew was the best meal he'd ever had.

The women remained quiet, Miss Winter taking up her seat near her sister. Miss Blanche produced a basket of mending while the elder sister watched him unabashedly.

He must be quite the sight, appearing on their door out of nowhere. It didn't look as though they had visitors often.

At last he finished the stew, and he began to tear pieces off the bread and pop them into his mouth. Warmed by the fire and food, he ate more slowly, glancing around the room. The walls of the cottage were plain, mostly stone with a few beams of wood supporting them here and there. There was the barest shelf above the fire, where a few chipped mugs and dried flowers rested. Despite the obvious poverty of the women, their dwelling was clean and didn't speak of neglect. For all the home was simple, it was comfortable.

Caspar tucked the last morsel of bread in his mouth, grateful it was thick and hearty. It would tide him over until morning.

"There now, Captain," Mrs. Michaelson said, resting her hands in her lap. "You are fed and rested. Tell us, how did you come to be in our woods? An Englishman wandering about alone, in the coldest parts of France, must certainly be suspect."

Caspar had prepared answers for anyone curious enough to ask about his presence in the war-torn country, but he could not resist his first words. "As suspect as three Englishwomen, obviously from a genteel background, living in the middle of a forest?" He grinned when she made no answer, though she appeared amused. "I am searching for something that was lost in these woods during the war. I feel duty bound to retrieve it."

"Something lost?" Miss Winter asked, arching one eyebrow and leaning forward. "Such as what?

And how would you expect to locate anything here in winter?"

"By careful searching," he said, edging around the question. "Why did your family decide to stay in France after the war?"

Miss Winter drew back and crossed her arms, pulling her deep red shawl tighter about her as she did. "We rather like it here," she said, lifting her chin.

The grandmother chuckled, drawing his eyes back to her lined and gentle face. "We all have our secrets, Scarlett. This man may keep his as well as we keep ours."

"Thank you for your understanding, Mrs. Michaelson." Caspar bowed as much as he could from his place on the floor, then raised his hand to cover a wide yawn. "My apologies," he said as soon as he'd recovered. "It has been a very long day."

"I can well imagine. Searching about for anything in this weather could only lead to fatigue. And—" the grandmother broke off to cough into a handkerchief.

Then the sudden howl of the wind brought all their attention to the door. The quiet Miss Blanche rose and went to the door, unbolting it to peer into the night. Cold air slipped through the crack, whipping around the room. The young woman leaned against the door to close it, fighting the wind.

"It's turning into a blizzard," she announced, her voice deeper than he'd expected, her words flat.

The grandmother put her hands down on either side of her chair and pushed upward, and Miss Winter moved to aid her, arm going around the older woman's shoulders.

"We must settle where you will sleep, Captain," the old woman said. "We have beds in the next room, if you wish—"

Caspar hurried to his feet, thinking of how his mother would despair of his manners. "Thank you, Mrs. Michaelson, but I will not take the beds of gentlewomen such as yourselves. I will be well enough out here, if you but leave me these blankets."

"Of course, Captain. You are most welcome. We will bid you goodnight."

Miss Blanche hurried ahead of her grandmother and sister, obviously keen to be out of his sight.

Miss Winter spoke, a smile on her face. "Good night, Captain Graysmark."

He bowed to her as well, a lower and more courtly gesture. "And to you, Miss Winter."

Her lips twitched upward but she said no more, helping her grandmother. The door eased shut behind them. Caspar looked around the room, gathering up the quilts and one small cushion to make his bed before the fire. Grateful for the shelter, and weary from the day, he fell into a doze, thinking of the looted French gold lost in the woods.

Scarlett shifted in the bed she shared with Blanche, unable to sleep despite the lateness of the hour. Her mind lingered on the stranger, the British captain, and his mysterious presence in their forest. His evasive answers to her questions left her less than satisfied and yet she trusted he would do them no harm.

There was something about his mannerisms, the gentle look in his eyes, that made her feel they were safe. Blanche hadn't experienced the same feelings, as she'd quietly pushed the trunk from the foot of their bed to sit before the door. Then again, of the two of them, Blanche often exercised more sense.

Rolling onto her side, Scarlett stared through the darkness at the shuttered window in the bedroom. In the summer, they'd left it open to let a breeze come through and she'd been able to see the stars.

On nights such as this, she missed the little things of her previous life, such as glass-paned windows. It would've soothed her soul if she could glimpse the night sky. Yet she must remain grateful, as Blanche always reminded her, that they had so many other things they could've lost. Like Grandmother, and each other, and this tiny cottage where no one knew to come looking for them. The French couldn't come pillage and plunder this cottage as they had the chateau her father had taken such pride in. And the English couldn't chase them off the land for treason.

Blanche rolled over and sighed when Scarlett huffed at the memory of being driven from both of their past homes.

"Scarlett," Blanche whispered. "You are making it impossible to sleep."

Chagrined, Scarlett snuggled deeper into the blankets. "I apologize. I cannot seem to be still."

"Are you thinking of that man out there?" Blanche asked, sounding disapproving. "We don't know a thing about him. I hope he leaves in the morning."

A howl of wind against the cottage shook the eaves. "He may not be able to leave. The storm is only getting worse."

"I don't trust him," Blanche whispered. "Why wouldn't he tell us what he is looking for?"

Though Scarlett had been thinking similarly, she immediately rose to the captain's defense. "He said he was looking for something he'd lost during the war. I think it must simply be a private matter. Perhaps he lost a personal object, or something that has military importance. It is none of our business."

Blanche turned away, pulling the blankets up higher. "It ought to be if he's sleeping in our house."

"On our floor," Scarlett pointed out. "He's been nothing but a gentleman."

"Hm. Thus far." Blanche yawned. "Go to sleep, Scarlett. If it *is* a blizzard, we will have work to do tomorrow."

Scarlett curled her toes in her wool stockings, already thinking of the biting cold work in the morning. They would have to go out and clear paths from the front door to the outhouse. Someone would have to check on the chickens in their little coop and the goat who supplied their milk, too. The morning chores would take hours, all of them spent in the frigid snow.

Perhaps Captain Graysmark would be willing to assist. He looked to be a strong gentleman. Clearing snow might not be as difficult for him as it was for someone of her size. And he wouldn't get nearly as cold wearing that massive fur coat. Smiling to herself, she closed her eyes and pictured the bearded Englishman going about doing all her chores for her. Perhaps if she was more educated in the feminine arts of flirtation, she could convince him to assist her.

The thought made her grin in the darkness and she almost laughed at herself. One thing her time in the forest had taken from her was her ability to be a genteel woman. She doubted she had any sort of talent to attract a man anymore.

Her hands were rough from work, her skin browned from being out in the sun, and her clothing was worn, drab, and more reminiscent of a sixteenth-century peasant than a young lady going to a ball.

Eventually, she drifted into dreams of ballrooms, where she wore a dress of spun gold. The only odd thing about it was that her partner was a large black bear. The large creature danced with as much grace as a gentleman, and she knew she was safe with him.

Chapter Three

Rising with the sun had grown into a habit for Caspar. Even when he found himself asleep on a woven rug, the only thing between him and a dirt floor. The room was dark yet, but the sounds of the storm were no longer present. Feeling around in the shadows, Caspar found his boots and dry socks. He was dressed in minutes and out the door. It opened inward, fortunately, as the snow had drifted up at least two feet.

Stepping out, he started pushing it out of the way with his boots. He shuffled through the snow toward the shed. The goat he'd seen the previous night would need attention, which meant one of the young ladies required a path to care for the animal.

After seeing to his horse, Caspar looked about the crisp white landscape for anything he might do to ease the load of the women who had sheltered him for a night.

Before long, Caspar had cleared a path from the front door to the shed, then he'd found a chopping block and several logs in need of splitting. He learned how to cut logs during his first winter on the Continent, a winter he'd rather not think about.

Caspar shrugged out of his fur coat and slung it over a low branch, then sought out the ax in the shed where he'd glimpsed several tools hanging on the wall. Tromping back and forth in the snow warmed him, everywhere except in his boots.

Once he began swinging the ax, he didn't even feel the cold. It was methodical work, the ax falling again and again to split a dozen logs, the sort of work to let a man think while he was at it.

Mostly, facing towards its eastern wall, he thought of the women inside the cottage. If his answers to the dark-haired Miss Winter were evasive, hers were positively slippery.

I am not here to puzzle out three helpless women in the forest. Caspar huffed at himself and swung the ax. *I am here to find the missing loot to return it to the people of this war-blighted land.*

The blue-gray light of dawn changed into the warm yellow glow of morning. The rhythmic swoosh and thunk of the ax as it found its mark filled his ears, and the rest of the world remained muted by the fallen snow. It was almost peaceful.

He'd thought the same thing the morning after his first French snow. The battlefield lay before his company, white and untouched. It hadn't taken long for the men on both sides to churn up the snow, leaving filth and blood in place of the gentle swells of white drifts.

Caspar paused long enough to wipe the sweat from his brow with the back of his jacket sleeve, and his eyes glimpsed movement along the side of the house. A splash of wine-red moved against the gray walls of the cottage, then into the snow. One of the women wore a shawl covering her head and shoulders as she made her way to the shed.

I'd wager that's the one called Scarlett. Caspar shook his head, thinking on the woman's fiery eyes and teasing smile. The name suited her well, given what he'd already seen of her personality and spirited wit.

He heaved the ax up, splitting the last of the logs he'd prepared. He bent and gathered several in his arms, intending to move them to the side of the house where he'd seen the wood stacked. There was enough to see the ladies through several weeks, easily, but giving them more hours of warmth and light felt like the least that he could do to return their kindness.

After stacking the wood, he hefted the ax and took it back to the shed.

Standing outside the door, he heard a gentle voice humming within and stopped. It was a melody he'd heard before, but he could not place it. The song was lilting, almost joyful.

Pushing the door open, Caspar peered inside the tiny space where his horse pressed against the shared wall of the cottage, content to chew at oats and straw. On the other side of the little room, nearly to where its thin planks sloped into the ground, was the gray goat and Miss Winter, filling a pail of milk.

The goat saw him first and bleated, then turned its head away as though it couldn't be bothered with him. Caspar chuckled, and Miss Winter's humming stopped.

"Good morning, Captain," the young woman said, her rosy lips quirking upward. "Thank you for clearing my path to Duchess." She nodded to indicate the title belonged to the goat, which struck him as oddly appropriate.

"You are most welcome. I am sorry if I disturbed Duchess with my entry." He pretended to bow to the goat, eliciting a larger grin from Miss Winter.

"She is a haughty creature, isn't she?" the woman said. "But she knows her worth." Miss Winter sat back on her three-legged milking stool and gave the goat a gentle pat. "We would be lost without her."

The slight curl of French to Miss Winter's English words added a measure of charm to everything she said and made him feel far too rough to exchange pleasantries with her. There'd always been something of a slight rasp to Caspar's voice since his youth.

"I wonder, Miss Winter, if there is a shovel I might use to clear more paths for you ladies to use?

The snow is deep in some places, which will not make it easy to move about in long skirts."

Lifting her bucket, Miss Winter moved toward him, meaning he had to back out into the cold. She spoke as she went, as though unaware of their close quarters. "The shovel is hanging up inside, in case we get snowed in. I would welcome a path to the necessary, and to the hen house, and our well."

"Excellent. I thought you might demure and tell me I had done enough." Caspar hoped she heard the teasing in his voice and held his hand out for the bucket, which Miss Winter gave him without hesitation.

She met his eyes with a solemn look in the brown depths of her own. "Captain, that would be the height of foolishness. We are three women, used to fending for ourselves. I could clear the path, as I have dozens of times, but when a man appears from the woods as if by magic and offers his aid, I will take it." She gestured for him to precede her back to the cottage, but he shook his head and held his hand out to indicate she must go first.

With a Gallic shrug of her shoulders, Miss Winter led the way. "And you shouldn't worry about so many formalities," she said, her voice carrying through the cold air back to him. "We are poor women living outside of civilization. I would rather be Scarlett than *Miss Winter*." There was a touch of authority in her voice when she bid him to call her by her Christian name.

"My mother taught me to behave like a gentleman and treat all women as ladies," he answered as they paused before the front door.

Scarlett turned to him, tilting her chin up the better to meet his eyes. "You do her a great credit, I am certain. But this is not England, and I am hardly nobility. Being formal is only a painful reminder of what once was, Captain. Please consider my request." She dropped a curtsy as though to illustrate her point, the graceful movement at odds with her old clothing and scuffed boots. She opened the door behind her and stepped backwards into the cottage.

"Blanche, the captain would like the use of the shovel," she said. Her eyes sparkled with what must be mischief.

An intriguing woman.

"Let the poor man eat some porridge before he goes out again." The grandmother was seated at the table, ladling out whitish gruel into bowls upon the table. "And bring the preserves, Scarlett. Our guest deserves something sweet to thank him for the work he's already done."

Caspar approached the table and lifted the pail. "Where would you like Duchess's offering, Mrs. Michaelson?"

"Over there, in that hutch. Blanche, please show the captain."

The fair-haired young woman's expression showed little of what she thought, but her almost hasty movement conveyed some discomfort in his presence. He didn't entirely blame her, of course. He hardly looked like the earl he was, unshaven and unwashed for far too long. Any woman would see him coming and think him a wild man.

After securing the goat's milk, Caspar came to the table, and Scarlett sat beside him on the roughhewn bench. The woman put a small crock down on the table between them and raised one of her eyebrows.

"Our finest wild-berry jam, Captain," she said with an air of presenting a great prize.

Blanche sat down across from them, lips pressed together and avoiding eye contact. He looked to the grandmother to see her smiling fondly about the table before she spoke to him as a gracious hostess.

"Captain, we are most grateful you found our home last night, as you have proven the very best of guests."

Though it was humble praise, it still made Caspar's ears go warm and he was grateful the beard hid some of his blush. As an experienced soldier, and a lord, he ought not to be so easily touched. But Mrs. Michaelson spoke with more gentility in her voice than many a London hostess, and he could feel the weight of her compliment.

"You are most kind, Mrs. Michaelson. Thank you for providing breakfast."

Scarlett opened the crock and spooned out purple jam into her bowl, then she held it out to him to do the same. "I hope it fills you up, Captain."

Caspar stared down into her lovely face, noting the flecks of gold in her eyes and the way her long, dark lashes brushed against her cheeks when she blinked.

He reached for the crock, taking it from her with both hands, his fingers briefly covering hers. He could easily envelope both her hands in one of his. But what surprised him was the way the warmth from her skin seemed to trickle into his hands, then up his arms, and throughout his body.

Her eyes widened as though she sensed him drawing the heat from her, then she snatched her hands back, leaving him to grasp the crock more firmly to keep it from dropping.

"Thank you." He turned from her and felt her lean away from him.

Whatever had passed between them in that brief touch had startled Caspar enough that he didn't blame her for being wary. The moment their fingers brushed, it was as though a connection had been formed between them. But what it meant, he didn't know. And he shouldn't care.

He had a treasure to find, after all.

Chapter Four

After the strange moment with the jam, Scarlett tried to avoid Caspar, which wasn't too difficult given that he was outside working and she was inside checking over the last of their winter stores. The cottage had a small root cellar, low and dark, which she disliked. She couldn't stand to her full height inside, nor could Blanche. But they both went down, Blanche with a lantern and Scarlett with a slate and chalk, to count up their root vegetables and jars of boiled chicken and pickled eggs. With an additional mouth to feed, Grandmother wanted to be certain of what remained to see them through the end of winter.

Jam is an odd thing to inspire such discomfort. Scarlett bit her bottom lip as she thought the moment over yet again. Had the captain felt that odd sort of humming in his blood when they touched, as she had?

"You shouldn't encourage him," Blanche murmured, startling her sister from her thoughts, after giving Scarlett the number of carrots dangling from the ceiling.

Scarlett marked the number on the slate and didn't even look up. "I don't know what you mean. I am only being myself. And encourage him to do what, exactly? Sleep on our floor? Clear our paths for us?" She cocked her head to one side and took in Blanche's disapproving frown.

"To be so familiar," her sister said. "The way you two jest with one another and act as though you are old friends instead of strangers is odd. I cannot think it advisable, given how little we know about him."

Although she'd rather dismiss her sister's concerns as out of hand, Scarlett couldn't deny the wisdom in Blanche's words.

"I can try, I suppose, to be more circumspect." Scarlett adjusted the slate in her hand and nodded. "How many onions are in the baskets?"

Blanche didn't appear overly impressed with her concession, but she went back to counting the onion bulbs. Scarlett marked down each number given, attempting to keep her mind on the task at hand and not the handsome stranger clearing their paths of snow. If he were a villain, wouldn't he have had plenty of opportunity to show his true nature? To take advantage of them?

After Blanche and Scarlett finished their accounting of the root cellar, Grandmother set them the task of baking bread.

"We must have enough for ourselves and to feed the captain," she told them, dusting the top of their table with flour.

Bread making was often an all-day task as they kneaded the loaves, let them rise, and kneaded them again. The work left her arms tired and her shoulders stiff, but as Blanche joined in with no objections, Scarlett couldn't justify giving voice to her complaints.

Really, she shouldn't have any. She ought to be grateful for all she had.

But I want more than this paltry existence, she thought, her knuckles deep in bread dough. *I miss our beautiful house and gardens, I miss going to parties and balls. I miss Father—*

Her eyes stung with tears, and she continued her work with her head down, hiding her red-rimmed eyes from her sister and grandmother. Blanche would lecture if she caught Scarlett even appearing less than content. Grandmother would grow gentle and sad. Neither response was wished for and so both were avoided by Scarlett's continual smile and forced bravery.

The dough properly prepared, Scarlett covered the bread with a clean cloth and set it in the little alcove near the fire to rise. Then, not looking to Blanche, she untied her apron strings, wiped her hands, and left the cottage. She took her shawl off the hook near the door as she went, wrapping it snuggly over her head and shoulders.

Going around the corner of the house at speed on the packed snow, Scarlett might've run headlong into the captain if he hadn't been large enough to look like a wall coming at her. She didn't stop, though she raised her hand in greeting, not yet trusting her voice.

He reached out as she made to walk around him in the higher snow. "Miss Winter," he said, his voice sounding like a growl when lowered. "Is something wrong?"

His gloved hand on her sleeve, wrapped around her wrist, was gentle. She could've easily pulled away. But Scarlett stayed where she was, looking down at the leather encased fingers. Her own hands were bare and would soon be cold.

"I forgot my mittens," she said, her voice a whisper.

He removed his hand and she immediately missed the connection between them, but then he wordlessly stripped the gloves from his hands. The captain held them out to her, and she followed the length of his arms up to his broad shoulders, then dared raise her gaze to his.

The deep blue eyes, making her think of summer skies, drew her in. Despite the dark, scruffy beard, everything about the man was noble. Scarlett clutched at the front of her shawl, twisting her fingers in the wool.

"I cannot take your gloves, Captain."

"Please. I've finished my work for now." His smile flashed from behind his whiskers and he held them a little closer. "Your fingers will freeze without them, Scarlett."

The way he said her name, adhering to her wish for less formality, almost startled her. Swallowing the emotions which had propelled her from the cottage, Scarlett nodded and held a hand out, to receive his generous offer.

Instead, the Englishman held one glove open and slid it over her hand, allowing her to wiggle her fingers into each appropriate compartment. Then he held out the other one to repeat the ritual.

The gloves were too large for her, of course, but they retained the heat of his hands. Scarlett looked down at them, seeing the fine quality of the stitching and feeling the warmth of wool inside, though the outer layer was smooth leather.

"Thank you, Captain."

"Caspar," he said, voice quiet. He didn't move, though the intimacy of knowing his name made her feel as though they stood much, much closer. "Why were you crying, Scarlett?"

At last she raised her eyes to his, the tremble returning to her bottom lip. "It is of no consequence."

Caspar looked about them until he spotted the felled tree near the edge of their cleared land. "Come, sit with me a moment. The rest will do us both some good, I think." He started tromping towards the log, his feet sinking into the snow. "Step where I step," he said over his shoulder.

Feeling rather ridiculous, Scarlett followed, lifting her skirts enough to make the wide steps more feasible. She went into the snow nearly up to her knees, but kept going until she reached the log, which he busily brushed clean with the sleeve of his coat.

"There," he declared, bowing and raising his hand with a flourish. "Your couch, my lady."

Scarlett bit her lip to keep from giggling at his presentation of the old dead tree, then lifted the corner of her skirt as best she could with the oversized gloves and curtsied.

"Thank you, kind sir." She sat, the cold seeping through her dress and quilted petticoat. Caspar sat down beside her, tucking his hands beneath his arms and gazing about as though their small clearing was a view worth taking in.

"It's amazing, isn't it?" he said, his rumbling voice sending a little thrill down her spine. "The way snow blankets everything in white, changing a landscape. What does this place look like in the spring, I wonder?"

"It looks muddy," she answered, thinking of the days after the thaw began when it was easier to go about barefoot than let her boots get stuck in the wet earth. "Especially where we till our garden." She pointed to the rear of the cottage where an ungainly line of sticks thrust into the ground made up a fence. "But the trees are lovely. Some of them have flowers, though most just turn a shade of green that's almost yellow. The trees are my favorite part."

"Mm. I would likely agree with you. At my home, we have plum trees near the house that blossom. As a boy, I spent hours beneath them, watching the flowers sway." He sighed and stretched his legs out before him. "I hope I return home in time to see them. It's been many years since I've witnessed an English spring."

Scarlett could well remember such days, watching as the grass deepened in color and her mother's gardens bloomed. She'd only been thirteen when they left England, yet it called to her still in her dreams.

Almost as if he'd read the turn in her thoughts, Caspar bent toward her. "Would you like to tell me why you were upset a moment ago? If there is anything at all I can do to help—"

"There is nothing to be done." Scarlett forced a more pleasant expression onto her face. "I was wishing for the days before we came to this place, for what my life once was. It is of no matter. I know I ought to be grateful, to have my sister, my grandmother, this home, when so many have lost everything to the war. We are safe and warm on even the coldest evenings. That must be enough."

Caspar regarded her silently, the weight of his gaze a pleasant one, and then he shook his head. "It isn't wrong to miss the way things were, so long as you move forward in the present. Our memories are what make us who we are. Mourning the passing of what was lost is natural, but you must determine to continue living for the blessings you still possess."

Scarlett's breathing had slowed as she listened to his words, turning them over in her mind, wondering if he could be right. Blanche would have Scarlet forget her past and Grandmother never spoke of what had been. Scarlett had expected an expression of false sympathy from Caspar, or an agreement that she mustn't allow herself to be sad over what was in the past.

"That sounds very wise, Caspar." Scarlett took in the little cottage, watching smoke rise from the chimney. "And it makes me feel less foolish."

"Our emotions only make us foolish if we act on them poorly." When she looked at him from the corner of her eye, he shrugged. "My mother used to say that. When I was a young boy, my elder brother was forever tormenting me. He meant it in fun, but I didn't see it that way, and if I cried he mocked me. Said I was a little milk maid. That made it worse, and I'd go blubbering to our mother." He chuckled and leaned back, stretching his legs out before him in the snow. "She told me not to be ashamed of my tears."

"I don't think that's something most sons would hear," Scarlett said, curious. "And it looks as though her advice did not do you much harm. You still grew into a capable man."

"Do you think so?" he asked, his eyes twinkling at her. "Capable. That's quite the compliment."

Scarlett laughed, her melancholy forgotten for the moment. "I can hardly say much more about you. I cannot call you handsome, because that beard hides your face, though I suppose I might compliment your fine manners, were it not for you sitting in the middle of our rug with your bare feet last night. I feel certain such behavior is still frowned upon in most English parlors."

Caspar laughed, a full, throaty sound that rumbled through the clearing around them. "You're right, of course. My manners are inexcusable. Though someone told me such things aren't necessary in these particular woods."

The warmth of her fingers recalled at least one more compliment she might pay. "I will call you generous and chivalrous. Those are qualities which are always appreciated." She held up her hands to show him his own gloves. "You gave these up for a silly woman, after all."

That light in his eyes gentled and he reached out, squeezing one of her gloved hands. "Not a silly woman. A friend in need of kindness." He rose and bowed to her, as low as one might for a duchess. "If you will excuse me, I am off to see if there is more I can do to be useful before I take up my search once more."

He tromped away, using his footprints from before to make his steps easier, and when he made it back to the path he'd cleared she called out to him.

"What is it you're searching for, Caspar?"

He turned and regarded her in silence for a moment, then raised his hands. "What else? Buried treasure." He grinned and turned back to the house, leaving her to wonder if he could be serious.

Buried treasure?

Scarlett stayed out a little longer, not wanting to enter the cottage on Caspar's heels and subject herself to another of Blanche's well-meant lectures. Instead she enjoyed the silence of the woods behind her, only the occasional song of a bird breaking the peaceful quiet of the morning.

At least it will be spring soon.

Chapter Five

Carrying a load of wood inside, Caspar stacked it neatly in the box by the fire. The air smelled of fresh bread, and a pan of potatoes and carrots simmered over the fire. His stomach refrained from shaming him with further growls, but the meal certainly tempted him.

"We will be ready to eat shortly," Mrs. Michaelson said, as though she'd read his mind. "Captain, I hope you have considered staying another night. You have more than made up for our hospitality." She smiled at him from her seat at their small table, artfully closing the dough over what looked to be a hand-pie.

The day half over, it was tempting to take her up on the offer of shelter and the warmth of a fire. His mind conjured the image of Scarlett upon the tree outside, wrapped in her shawl and wearing his gloves, but Caspar shook his head.

"I need to be about my business, Mrs. Michaelson, but I thank you for the offer."

She nodded her understanding and wiped her hands on her apron. "Blanche, gather the captain's rations."

Miss Blanche went to the end of the table, where she took up a cloth bundle. She brought it to him and thrust it in his direction. Caspar couldn't be certain if the young woman was merely shy or if she genuinely disliked him. He spoke his thanks sincerely anyway and accepted the tied cloth.

"What is this?" he asked Mrs. Michaelson, untying the bundle.

"As I said, rations. I hope they will hold you over for a time. But know this, Captain Graysmark, if you wish to return to our fire for any reason you are always welcome."

Caspar peered inside, seeing small hand pies, a loaf of bread, cheese, and dried fruit. "Mrs. Michaelson, this is too much. I have my own rations, though they are admittedly less appetizing."

"Take it and say no more, Captain." Mrs. Michaelson's voice held compassion. "While I know not what you search for, I know it will be cold and lonely in the forest. I pray you stay well."

"Thank you. You have been a most generous hostess." Caspar bowed. "I will take my leave of you now, while the sun is still high."

He went to the shed and packed the food prepared for him, checking his saddle and belongings, and led his horse from the building out into the snow.

Scarlett appeared before him, her nose wrinkled and a frown on her lovely face. "You are leaving? Already?"

"I am afraid I must," he answered gently. Scarlett's head dropped, disappointment written plainly in her stiff posture. She stripped off his gloves and held them out to him.

"It was good to meet you, Captain," she said, her voice suspiciously tight.

Caspar reached out to take the gloves, but then he caught her bare hand instead. The gently bred girl hadn't asked to become a peasant. As with thousands of others, she'd fallen victim to wars not of her making. She ought to have been protected by a father, should have returned to family in England.

"Is there no one I may inform of your whereabouts?" Caspar asked in earnest. "A family friend, a relative? Surely there are people in England who would have you share their homes rather than live here, in the woods."

She studied his hand before slowly raising her head, the red-rims of her eyes causing his heart to ache for her. "There is no one who would have us, Captain. Not now, or ever."

It couldn't be true. Who wouldn't want this beautiful young woman with an infectious smile in their home?

"It's Caspar," he said, releasing his hold on her and tucking his hands into his gloves. "And don't forget, you have a friend in me if ever you wish to return."

A laugh escaped her, the sound at odds with the emotion in her eyes. "This sounds like a very permanent goodbye. Are you so certain of where to find your treasure?"

"Not entirely," he admitted. "I have wandered far off course. I cannot see that path leading me here again."

Scarlett wrapped her arms around herself, perhaps warding off the cold. "I understand. It was good to meet you, and I will never forget what you said about the past. Thank you."

Taking his leave from the cottage had been easily done, with few words and gestures, but somehow mounting and riding away with Scarlett watching was infinitely more difficult. They'd hardly spoken, but when he looked over his shoulder to offer one last wave and she remained where she had been, it stirred something in his breast.

Her hand, smaller than his but calloused by work, lifted and returned the wave just before he went down the little rise between the cottage and a stream, blocking Scarlett from view.

Caspar faced forward and gave his horse a pat along the neck. There weren't many daylight hours left and he must find where he'd lost the path the night before. But the further behind him the cottage fell, the more he wished he would have stayed one more night.

Chapter Six

Chickens in winter were, in Scarlett's mind, the laziest of creatures. They stayed in their little house, which smelled rather horrid, clucking and sitting upon their straw nests. They hardly stirred when she reached beneath them to see if any had bothered to lay eggs. They gave her enough baleful glances for her to know they resented the intrusion and the cold air she let in when she opened the human-sized door to their domain.

A handful of eggs in her basket, Scarlett left them gladly, easily stomping along the path cleared for her by Caspar the day before. The snow crunched beneath her scuffed boots, the familiar sound the only one at the moment. The sun had begun to dip beneath the horizon, the shadows of the forest trees painted dark blue lines across the clearing, and the temperature decreased with each passing moment.

Would Caspar be warm enough out in the forest? He had his massive fur coat, of course, and could build a fire. What if it snowed again, or sleeted? Though spring crept nearer with each passing day, the nights were still freezing. Perhaps it wouldn't matter. Perhaps he'd gone too far from them to even think of returning.

Scarlett stopped before the door and set her basket down, turning to look in the direction Caspar had disappeared.

"If I was a man," she whispered to the snowy hill, "I would go after him and find some adventure." But she wasn't a man. And if she had been, she knew she would still stay to look after her grandmother and sister.

Besides those points, half the reason she wished to follow Caspar had more to do with the fact that *he* was a man. A kind, strong gentleman. It had been too long since she'd been near such as he, which had to account for the way her heart had thrummed every time he spoke to her. Oh, she'd gone with Grandmother to the closest village, nearly half a day's walk away from the mountains, and seen a few of the men there. But they were a humble group of people, mostly farmers, and she'd never even been curious about them.

The sun fully disappeared behind the naked branches and hills, leaving her in the semi-darkness.

If ever Scarlett wished to marry, to have a husband to love and babies to tend to, she knew the farmers were the only option she had. There were no balls in her new world, no handsome gentlemen to send flowers or come calling. Those days were long past, and all her lessons on comportment, music, dancing, and languages were useless to the woman she'd become.

"I should try speaking Italian to the chickens," she muttered, lifting the egg basket. "They may appreciate it." Amused at the thought, Scarlett entered the cottage and shut the door upon the cold winter night.

"There you are, dear," Grandmother said, looking up from stirring the pot of dinner. "How are our biddies?"

"Perfectly well, and as conceited as ever." Scarlett's words remained light. She went to the hutch with her basket and began placing the eggs in a bowl. Blanche came out of the bedroom with another of their grandmother's shawls and laid it over her back.

Scarlett met her sister's eyes, asking a question. *Is something wrong?* They often held these silent conversations over their grandmother's head, her health the greatest concern to the sisters. Winter was difficult on the elderly woman, and if she grew sick, they would make poor nurses.

Blanche shook her head slightly and shrugged. Skirting the table, she took their bowls from the shelves and spoons from the cup in which they stood. She laid out their places, prompting Scarlett to hurry and lay out a basket of rolls. Their meager meal on the table, Grandmother took her seat while Blanche fetched the steaming pot of soup.

What would they do if something happened to Grandmother? She was the one who had taught them, that very first summer at the cottage, how to gather eggs, prepare a chicken to eat, and bake bread.

They hadn't been educated to be farmers or dairy maids, but their grandmother had been a merchant's daughter and recalled how to do such things. They'd worked for weeks to put the cottage and its garden in order, to mend the holes in the chicken house, and faced one disaster after another learning to make goat cheese.

But Grandmother had taught them, had walked to and from the village to ask questions of the people there, humbling herself to learn what she did not know for the sake of her granddaughters.

After the meal was over, Scarlett went back to her boots. She had to milk Duchess, and Blanche would tidy up after the meal. Scarlett paused at the door, taking in the simple room. Grandmother tottered back to her chair by the fire, using a cane they'd bartered for in the fall when they'd traded some of their excess vegetables in the village.

Though she missed what she'd once had, Scarlett found heeding Caspar's words made it easier to accept it was gone. The life she shared with Blanche and Grandmother might've been simple, but it was a good one.

Milking the goat never took long, but when Blanche unexpectedly entered the shed, Scarlett sat up in surprise.

"Is something wrong?" she asked.

Blanche crossed her arms tightly beneath her gray shawl. "No, but I wanted to speak to you about Grandmother. She's been very odd today. Have you noticed?"

Scarlett, in charge of most of the outdoor chores, hadn't. "I know she took a nap today, but that isn't so unusual of late."

"That's what worries me." Blanche came closer and leaned against the wall near Scarlett and Duchess. Her face had turned pale and dark half-circles underscored each of her eyes. "She grows tired too often. This life is hard on her. The work is too difficult and she is not young enough to recover from a cold day like this one. What do we do if she grows weaker, Scarlett?" Blanche's words dwindled to a whisper, echoing Scarlett's unspoken fears.

"I don't know." Scarlett rose and lifted the pail of milk with her. "But we will do our best to keep her well. If she grows ill, I could go to the village and see if the herb woman has any cures."

Blanche grimaced. "Why did this little piece of land have to be all we could afford? It's a cottage. In a forest." Blanche rubbed her forehead while Scarlett's eyebrows raised. She'd never heard her sister complain about their situation before. "There are no physicians out here."

Ah. That explained it. Blanche wasn't thinking of herself, but of Grandmother.

"Even if there were," Scarlett reminded her gently, "we don't have any way to pay a doctor."

Blanche closed her eyes and tilted her head back. "I know. Perhaps we could find one who liked goat cheese, though, and barter with him."

The absurdity of the comment struck Scarlett and she couldn't help the laugh that escaped her. Blanche narrowed her eyes and glared, but a smile turned her lips upward too.

"What we need," Scarlett said with one hand on her hip and the other gripping the pail of milk, "is a fairy godmother. Or a knight in shining armor."

"Instead we had a bear," Blanche muttered, turning to leave.

Caspar. Scarlett closed her eyes for a moment, picturing his bearded grin and bright blue eyes. If only he had stayed.

To what end? He hadn't seemed reluctant to leave. Her pathetic need for attention, for his company, was not explainable and not shared by him. In less than a day, he'd come into her life and gone out of it. She would have to accept that an impoverished family in the woods was of no interest to men such as he.

Chapter Seven

The road wasn't far from the cottage.

Caspar looked at the tracks in the road with interest, then back over his shoulder. It was, perhaps, five miles from Scarlett and the other ladies.

He shook his head and continued on, watching for markers he'd tried hard to remember when his lieutenant, Birks, had described them.

A smaller path, a game trail, should split from the road leading downhill. He was to follow that path to a stream, cross the water in a straight line, and over a hill he would find himself in a stand of trees. And somewhere in those trees, he would find the chest of looted funds hidden in a hollowed-out trunk, to return to the people from whom it had been stolen.

It hadn't seemed all that complicated in his head when he set out, though Birks had tried to warn him. The game trail may be lost if the animals stopped using it or obscured by the elements.

But I have to try. Caspar had followed the road until nightfall. *Too far. I'll have to go back down the road in the morning.*

For three days he went back and forth on the road, only seeing the occasional trapper with a wagon and one other traveler on a horse. Besides those on the road, he saw no tracks to indicate a habitual path of game.

On the fourth day, Caspar tried a different tact. He left the road to find the stream. If he found the stream, he might find a path leading away from it and could surmise from there where to go.

The problem with finding the frozen stream, however, was just that. The water was frozen and there was little evidence of animal activity around it.

Caspar made camp by the ice and ate the last of the rolls given him by Mrs. Michaelson. As he chewed on the slightly stiff bread, staring into his fire, he formed another plan.

If he remained long enough for the water to thaw and the animals returned to make use of the stream, he might have an easier time finding the hidden chest. The snow made everything difficult. While he was provisioned to camp out in the weather for a few more weeks, finding a roof to go over his head would make things much more comfortable.

And if a lovely young woman with fiery brown eyes and a teasing smile happened to be under the same roof—

His horse snorted, pulling him back into the present. Caspar rose and adjusted the animal's blanket and found a turnip he'd held back as a treat. After feeding Fortinbras, he went back to the fire.

Begging shelter of three women struck him as rather pathetic. They owed him nothing after the first night, and he could hardly return without good reason and a willingness to compensate them for their trouble. It wouldn't take more than half a day to return to the cottage in good weather.

Caspar pitched his small canvas tent and crawled inside, wishing it were possible to bring the fire in with him.

A place on a rug far outranked his current sleeping situation.

The night's lack of rest served to strengthen his resolve to go back. Trees creaked above him, the frozen stream made strange groaning sounds, and the wind found ways to slip into the tent to curl up against him before drifting out again.

By morning, Caspar made his decision.

I won't go back, stumbling through the door like a wild animal. He looked down at the sleeves of his fur coat as he broke camp, remembering Scarlett had likened him to a bear. He smirked to himself and dug around in one of his bags until he found his shaving kit.

"I can't do anything about the coat," he said to his horse, by way of explanation. He'd no intention of shaving until he reentered civilization, but the women of the stone cottage certainly deserved a similar sort of thoughtfulness. "But I can be rid of the beard."

His mother would've had a fit to see his whiskers grown out in such a manner.

Caspar took the mirror, smaller than his palm, and found an obliging tree limb to hold it at the right angle. He melted snow in a tin cup, then went to work.

The shave wasn't his best, and it took a great deal of time given the amount of hair and the tiny mirror. When the job was done to his satisfaction, Caspar finished breaking camp. He checked his rifle and loaded it, then mounted.

It was winter, after all, and unlike England, France still had wolves. Not to mention wild boar, and real bears. The scarcity of game he'd encountered thus far could mean there was a predator in the area getting desperate to eat.

No sooner did he have the thought, finding his way out of the trees, than a buck appeared before him. Instinct served Caspar, and he was able to get off a shot just as the animal took a leap to flee the way it had come. He dismounted and hurried to the deer, making certain it did not suffer.

As a young gentleman, he'd been on his share of hunts on his father's lands. But it was the servants who always bagged the birds and dressed the deer. Caspar wasn't entirely sure what to do with the animal, but he'd not let it go to waste. In the military, wild game was rarely seen, and if caught was kept secret to provide better food to the men who found it.

How many times had he come across Tomley, that shifty-eyed sergeant, eating birds that had obviously been taken from a farm? Hunger had driven many men to desperate acts, but Tomley always seemed to find himself food.

The whole of the morning was spent field-dressing the roe deer, an animal familiar to him despite his distance from home. By the time he'd finished, the sun had reached its highest point for a winter day. Caspar stowed his catch atop his horse and began again to the cottage.

With any luck, he'd arrive before dark.

Chapter Eight

The wind whistled through the trees, but the sound hadn't made Scarlett shudder since their first winter in the cottage. Mostly she wished she knew how to whistle back, to amuse herself by imitating the plaintive tune.

Giving Duchess a pat, Scarlett lifted the pail of milk and shuffled through the straw to the door of the shed. Out into the fading light she went, tilting her head back to look up at the first stars of the evening. Her breath came out in white puffs of air. She went around the house, concentrating on where she stepped. The packed snow had become slippery with her frequent use of it, and it would not do to spill all of Duchess's hard work.

A horse, or something that sounded like a horse, nickered in the distance. Scarlett froze, stilled her breathing, and listened.

Caspar?

No other sounds came to confirm the first, and the hilltop remained empty except for the bare trees.

She'd imagined his return.

Scarlett closed her eyes and allowed the humiliation to sink back into her breast.

Why would he come back here? There was no reason for him to return to their humble cottage and it was pure vanity to think he might have thought of them, of *her*, even once since leaving.

Determined not to glance in the direction of his departure, Scarlett made haste to enter the cabin, caring less about spilled milk.

Once inside, she removed her boots and took care of the milk. Tomorrow was cheese-making day. That gave her reason to smile. It wasn't a difficult process, and the results were delicious. They'd finally perfected a harder cheese, after they'd learned the secret of creating a rind with ash to protect the substance. Even the softer curds were delicious in soups and toasted on bread.

"Scarlett," Grandmother said from her place at the table. "Will you bring the berry pie to the table? I think it will go well with the meal tonight."

It was the same meal they'd had most winter nights. Stew and bread. The pie would be most welcome. Scarlett found the delicious pastry and brought it to the table. Blanche served everyone a bowl of vegetable stew.

A knock at the door sounded and Blanche gasped softly. "Twice in a week," she whispered, her eyebrows shooting up to the scarf she'd tied over her hair that day to protect it from dust while she cleaned.

Scarlett's heart thumped against her ribs nearly as loud as the knock had on the door.

Without waiting for her grandmother to bid her, Scarlett rose and hurried to put her hand to the bolt.

"Scarlett," Blanche hissed, bringing Scarlett to her senses. "It might not be the captain."

Flushing at her own eagerness, Scarlett nodded her understanding as she asked, voice pitched to carry through the wood, "Who is there?"

"A big, ugly bear," the answer came in Caspar's growly voice. "Might there be room at your table for me?"

Her cheeks flushed, her fingers tingled, and she slid back the bolt without waiting for anyone to speak another word. She opened the door inward and the light from their lamp and the fire bathed the man in a rich, golden glow.

And Scarlett quite forgot everything in the instant she saw his face, without its dark beard. His familiar blue eyes danced in the light, or else she might not believe it was Caspar before her. Without his beard, she could see he was not as old as she'd thought. His face was young and unlined. He had high cheekbones and a cleft at his chin. She could suddenly picture him in a soldier's uniform or dressed for a ball in London.

She clutched her red shawl more tightly around her, aware of the patch on her dress and its faded pattern.

His cheerful expression changed as she stared at him, from an almost teasing look to something more serious. "Miss Winter," he said, bowing slightly. "Won't you let an old friend inside?"

It was then she finally noticed he had a rather large bundle in his arms and it appeared he'd already put his horse in the shed.

Scarlett, with her face warm enough to prove her namesake, stepped aside to allow him entry. "Of course. Please come in, Captain."

"You've returned to us, Captain Graysmark," Grandmother said, sounding not at all surprised. "Welcome. And how punctual you are. We are serving dinner, sir. Will you not join us?"

"Thank you, Mrs. Michaelson. As to the punctuality, I am quite late. I'd hoped to arrive in time to add this to your table." He lifted the bundle. "Venison."

Blanche gasped aloud, startling Scarlett. Her younger sister came around the table with excited steps and hefted the bundle directly out of Caspar's arms.

"This is a blessing," she said, eyes wide and grateful. "Thank you, Captain. If you please, we will prepare some tomorrow. And the day after." She went directly to the root cellar, spots of color on her cheeks.

Scarlett stared after her sister in some perplexity.

"Had I known a gift of deer would get that reaction, I would've gone off hunting sooner," Caspar said, voice lowered for Scarlett's ears alone.

She looked up at him, the shyness not quite gone. As she'd hoped for days he would return, the sudden inability to speak to him was unsettling. He gave her a questioning glance but went to the basin where they washed their hands.

Blanche returned, cheeks still pink and a pretty smile on her face. They sat at the table on the mismatched chairs, and Grandmother spoke first.

"Did you find what you lost, Captain Graysmark?" she asked.

"Not yet." His admittance didn't sound regretful in the least, and his smile remained in place. "I think I will have an easier time of it when the snow melts."

"It's usually in March we start to see grass," Grandmother said sagely. "What is today, Scarlett?"

Time-keeping was one of Scarlett's duties, one which she enjoyed. "February seventeenth. Today is Tuesday."

Caspar stirred his stew, watching the steam rise from the bowl. "I was hoping I might beg for your hospitality, Mrs. Michaelson. I will contribute to the household, of course, through hunting and seeing to any chores that may be done. Is that an acceptable bargain to you?"

Grandmother sat straight in her chair and pursed her lips in thought. "Captain, if it was only myself in this cottage, I would say yes. But there are two young women present. Unmarried young women. We may be far from London society, but we are not far enough for me to be unconcerned on what your time here might mean for my granddaughters."

Heat rose in Scarlett's cheek and she looked across the table to where Blanche sat, whose reaction was to grow paler. Blanche dropped her eyes to her bowl of food, but Scarlett turned to see what Caspar made of her grandmother's words.

She could see the soldier in him, in the way he held his body stiff, and he spoke with an almost stern tone. "I fully understand you, Mrs. Michaelson. Your granddaughters' safety and reputations are safe with me, I swear on my honor. I would not betray your kindness in any way."

Grandmother looked from him to Blanche, then to Scarlett, where her eyes lingered as she spoke to them all. "You are welcome here." Her tone gentled considerably as she added, "As long as you mind your manners."

Caspar's smile appeared, more charming without the beard to hide so much of it. When he turned that smile in her direction, Scarlett warmed from her toes up to the tips of her ears.

I hope spring never comes. Scarlett's heart thudded merrily at the thought of a long, cold February.

Chapter Nine

The morning found Caspar stuffing his feet into his boots before the sun had a chance to rise. He ran his hands through his hair before rubbing at the scruff on his chin. He missed his batman. He'd had a clean shave most days in the military, as was befitting an officer. Some days he'd thought it a waste of time. The beard he'd allowed to grow on his journey to France had felt like a sort of freedom, until he'd been called a bear by an attractive young woman.

He snorted at himself and rose from the bench by the fire, going to the chair where he'd left his fur overcoat the night before.

The door to the women's bedroom opened, making him still. It was dark in the cottage, with the windows shuttered and the fire banked. At first he couldn't tell who it was, though he half-hoped it was Scarlett.

"Caspar? Are you awake?"

The way she'd stared at him the night before, as though she'd never seen him before, surprised and flattered him. The shaving might not be his favorite part of social grooming, but it may well be worth the effort. If she ever spoke to him again. Blanche had been the talkative one at the dinner table, even if she spoke of nothing more than her plans for the venison he'd brought them.

"Scarlett." He grinned in the dark, but hastily reminded himself of her grandmother's caution. Mrs. Michaelson wanted to protect the girls from any pain he may cause them. Forming attachments with a woman, then leaving her behind, would give pain to all of them.

She joined him near the table, her presence soothing in the silent chill of the room. He heard the rustle of her clothes, then the sound of flint struck, and then a candle burned on the table. Scarlett stood a mere foot from him, twisting the ends of her shawl.

"Good morning," he said, keeping his voice low in case the other ladies remained asleep. Scarlett was dressed in a plain gray gown. She seemed to have two, one gray, one faded blue. Her stockinged feet peeked from beneath the hem.

"Good morning." Her words brought him back to the study of her face, half in shadow. "Would you like something to eat?" she asked. "Something to drink before you go out into the cold?"

"Yes, thank you. To tell the truth, I'm not even certain what I'm going to do out there. Maybe you might offer me some direction as well as food and drink?" he asked, trying to tease a smile from her.

It worked, and her eyebrows rose along with the corners of her mouth. "Oh dear. A hired man who doesn't know what he's been hired to do."

Caspar nearly jested that she'd found her tongue again but refrained. There was no reason to risk upsetting her and losing her cheerful conversation. "Might I do anything to help you?"

She shook her head and moved to the hutch. "Only sit, Caspar, and let me be cook and footman." He watched as she put a kettle on a hook over the fire, stirring it back to life, then produced bread, jam, and started cracking eggs into a flat-bottomed pan. She moved with surety in her tasks, but also a grace he couldn't recall ever seeing a servant display.

He said nothing for a time, content to watch her work.

"What was your upbringing like, Scarlett, that you can speak English, French, and cook a man his breakfast?" he asked after some minutes passed.

She hesitated over the pan of eggs before taking it in hand and bringing it to the table. "It was a good one, I should think." Her hands smoothed down her beige apron before she returned for the kettle, swinging the hook out from the fire and grasping the handle with a towel. "I had a dancing master, a painting master, a music instructor, a German tutor, and my parents spoke French to me, as did everyone around me. Grandmother spoke English." She poured the hot water from the kettle into a teapot.

"You have a myriad of accomplishments, then." He still couldn't understand why they lived in the forest. Why a life of solitude instead of staying in a village, or town? Why not seek positions that would make use of all she knew? "What of the cooking?"

"Preparing eggs is hardly cooking. I think I could make them in my sleep." She served him a pile of yellow, fluffy eggs on a plate with his bread and jam. A moment later she had a mug next to him, the smell rather bitter. "Tea is too dear for us, but we do have some coffee. If you'd like, a little goat's milk is just the thing for it."

"Is it?" he asked, looking up into her eyes. How many women of his acquaintance boasted a formal education like hers? Several, he should think, but he couldn't imagine even one of them setting his breakfast in front of him like a servant. It took a special kind of resilience and determination to move from one life to another.

Until he'd been in the army for several months, he'd felt certain he could never make such a change. But when the enemy fire tore through a duke's son and a cobbler's son with equally disastrous results, Caspar's perspective altered.

Scarlett fetched the goat's milk and poured it from a clay pitcher into his cup.

What would she look like, holding his mother's favorite teapot? If she held the delicate cup that matched in her hand, and wore a gown of fine muslin, would it add to her beauty?

"Thank you." Caspar cleared his throat and tried to clear his mind as well. Giving his attention to his food, he tried to ignore the strange stirring in his heart.

Scarlett didn't sit to eat with him, though he wished she had. Instead she moved about, gathering a host of objects at the other end of the table. Twine, thin cloths, bowls, and more milk. She began her work by the light of the single candle and he watched, fascinated, as she filled a cloth with a white, thick substance. She pulled the edges of the cloth together and used the twine to hold it together, like a sack.

"You appear very perplexed, Captain," she said, laughter in her voice. "Have you never seen a woman make cheese before?"

Caspar chuckled and met her eyes, liking the spark in them. "I cannot say that I have, Miss Winter." But now that he had, he rather enjoyed the sight.

Sounds in the other room alerted him that the other women were stirring. He swallowed another bite of bread and washed it down with the coffee, warmth flooding him.

"Scarlett, what chores might I do for your family today?"

She didn't look up from her work, though her brow puckered in thought. "The animals need to be fed. Blanche usually does that in the mornings, but I know she would appreciate your help so she can start on the venison. With your horse in the shed it will need more mucking and fresh straw laid out. Is that enough to begin?"

"It is." Caspar finished his breakfast and went for his coat. It felt odd, walking out on her. While she did the chores of a farmer's wife, Scarlett's upbringing and mannerisms declared her a lady. "I will return for more work later, Miss Winter." He bowed, but this time with all seriousness.

She smiled at him over her bowls and dipped a curtsy appropriate for an English parlor. "Thank you, Captain Graysmark."

Caspar went into the cold with a light heart.

Chapter Ten

Scarlett, wrapped in shawl and mittens, shuffled through the snow with her empty pails. It was her turn to fetch water from the well. Melted snow worked nearly as well, in her opinion, but Blanche insisted it didn't taste as nice as what came from the ground.

The well's bucket was in fine shape, as was the rope that held it. She flung the wooden bucket down into the dark well as hard as she could, and a satisfying crack told her she'd managed to break the ice below. Turning the hand crank, Scarlett began to pull the water back out.

Something about the morning encounter with Caspar had been different; the peace hanging in the air between them an almost tangible thing. When he'd left to search out his treasure, she'd grown lonely and empty without good reason. At his return, things were somehow even more upside down.

Scarlett couldn't deny her attraction to him, but he was the first gentleman she'd seen up close in years. Was it merely lack of practice or desperation that made her heart race when he appeared on their doorstep? Why had every word he spoke that morning felt like a whispered secret, just for her?

Scarlett nearly snorted. *I am little better than a hermit if I take the words he said this morning for anything more than what they were—simple conversation.*

The bucket appeared and she reached out to grab it, pulling it to rest on the wall of the well. She tipped it, filling her two smaller pails.

A branch snapped on the hill behind her, and an icy awareness raised the hair on her arms.

Animals in the forest made plenty of noise. She'd laid awake many night listening to the comings and goings of owls, deer, and curious boar. And such creatures didn't snap twigs that way.

Remaining calm, her eyes swept the clearing for a sign of Caspar. If she couldn't see him, perhaps he was the one on the hill. But there he was, stepping out of the shed with a pitchfork full of hay for the compost pile.

She sucked in a breath and moved as normal, bending to lift both pails in her hands. As she did so, with the well for cover, she peeked over her shoulder.

Nothing moved behind her.

Scarlett started back to the cottage. She took the pails all the way to the door, where she left them in the snow. She went to Caspar. He looked up from his work, sweat on his brow despite the cold day, his fur coat nowhere to be seen.

"Scarlett? Is something wrong?" He straightened and held out his hand, then hastily lowered it.

"I think there's a man in the forest. Watching the cottage." She wrapped her arms around herself. "Up on the hill."

Caspar didn't even glance in the direction she indicated, which made her admire him still more. He spoke earnestly, his rich voice soothing her at once. "I'll go to the back of the cottage and slip into the trees myself, circling around. Go inside, bolt the door, and don't come out until you know I have returned."

That he took her seriously eased the tension in Scarlett's shoulders. She reached out a mittened hand, resting it on his forearm. "If it is a beggar, bring him closer so we can feed him. But please, Caspar, be careful."

His blue eyes glittered down at her and his smile turned softer. "You worry about me, do you?"

She felt the blush creep into her cheeks. "Of course, I do. You are doing all my difficult chores for me, after all." She squeezed his arm, and his hand came up to rest over hers. The heat from his touch seared her through the wool mitten.

"I will be careful, my dear, and save you from cleaning up after the horse and goat." He spoke with sincerity and a sort of understanding that made the silly words sweet. He then set the pitchfork over his shoulder and went around the shed, swinging his free arm as he walked, as though he meant to see about work on the other side of the cottage.

Scarlett gathered her shawl close and retrieved her pails. Once inside, she shut and bolted the door.

Grandmother was in bed, taking an afternoon nap, but Blanche was at the table reading their worn copy of Shakespeare's *Hamlet*. Not at all cheerful reading, by Scarlett's way of thinking, but their choices were rather limited.

"I have some venison in the pot," Blanche said, without looking up from her book. "Do you think we ought to have potatoes and onions or mushrooms and carrots? I cannot make up my mind, except that we will *not* have the radishes."

Agitated, Scarlett paced from the door to the table and back, mumbling an answer even she wasn't certain of.

Blanche spoke, drawing Scarlett's attention to her. "Scarlett? You always have an opinion about onions." Blanche's voice was light, trying to tease a response from her inattentive sister.

"Carrots and mushrooms, then," Scarlett answered, turning back to the door. If only they had glass-paned windows!

The sound of the chair scraping back over the earthen floor told her Blanche was coming nearer. "Scarlett?"

"There might be a man out in the forest," Scarlett said at last, looking down at her boots. She ought to have taken them off rather than walk around the house in them, muddying things. "Casp—The captain went to check."

"Oh." Blanche's eyebrows drew down. "The captain is a soldier, Scarlett. I'm certain all will be well."

The reminder of Caspar's profession didn't soothe her at all. "Even soldiers can be ambushed."

Blanche studied Scarlett with a shrewd look. "You care about Captain Graysmark."

"Yes. Don't you?" Scarlett turned away to hide the tell-tale blush in her cheeks.

"Perhaps you better find out more about what he's searching for, Scarlett. Maybe whoever is out there is one of his friends, or at least looking for the same thing." Blanche turned and walked away, shaking her head with obvious impatience. "A handsome face doesn't mean he is a good man. Have you told him about our family? If he knew, he might not be so happy to stay in a cottage with traitors to the Crown."

Closing her eyes, Scarlett fought against the wisdom in her sister's words. She didn't care what Caspar was searching for. An honorable man such as he wouldn't be in the woods for a dishonorable purpose. But then, would such a man continue to associate with her if he learned the real reason they stayed in France, hidden from everyone?

She didn't want to know the answer. She didn't have to. Caspar would be gone in a matter of weeks and she'd likely never see him again.

But then, there was another man in the woods she may have to worry over. Scarlett shuddered, hoping for Caspar's safety and worrying over her own.

Chapter Eleven

As captain of a company tasked with undertaking clandestine assignments, Caspar had done his fair share of sneaking around in the woods. He wasn't a spy, by any means, but he could move quietly enough to observe without being observed.

Caspar made his way through the trees, a hand hovering near the pistol he'd tucked into his belt. The women in the cottage lived far enough away from main paths and roads that no one could easily stumble upon them, but a hunter may well have seen the home and stopped to investigate it.

Caspar trusted Scarlett's instincts. She'd lived in the cottage for several years, from what he could tell. And there were times a person could simply sense such things.

Birds sang in the distance, but all was still where he crept through the trees. Likely he was viewed as a predator by any wildlife nearby. But the stillness meant slinking along with care.

Finally, he saw sign in the snow of someone else. The footprints were smaller than his own, but the shape would not match either of the young women's shoes.

Someone had been walking along the hill, just below its crest on the side opposite from the cottage. The boot prints weren't too deep; the person was slight. Narrowing his eyes, Caspar studied the places the boots were deepest. That was when the man had been watching the cottage.

Moving more cautiously, Caspar followed the prints for some time, but they led onto a rocky outcropping, and Caspar had been gone too long to continue tracking the stranger.

He withdrew from the search, returning to the cottage with a troubled mind. Someone had spied on the cottage. Would that person return another time or had it been idle curiosity that made him linger? If the man saw Caspar, had he decided it wasn't worth making any trouble?

Whatever the case, it unsettled Caspar that someone had stood watching Scarlett. If he hadn't been at the cottage, the women would be quite helpless in the face of a man with ill intent. Three women living alone in the forest tempted fate in the worst of ways.

He arrived back at the cottage and called out, as soon as he was near enough for his voice to carry. "I have returned, ladies. There is nothing in the woods to trouble you today."

The door opened and Scarlett stood inside, framed by the gray stone doorway. Caspar stopped for a moment, admiring the scene despite his worry. The snow blanketing the world in white, the gray stone cottage with its black shuttered windows, and a beautiful woman welcoming him in, her red shawl the only bright splash of color.

If I were an artist, this would be a moment worthy of a masterpiece.

Scarlett's shoulders sagged, and she wore an expression of relief. "You were gone for half an hour at least."

"Let the man in so he can warm up," Blanche's voice called from inside.

Caspar chuckled and paused before stepping inside, gazing into Scarlett's upturned face. "Thank you for worrying after me."

She blushed prettily and stepped aside, allowing him entrance. He moved carefully past her and into the cottage, where he took his seat at the table, wondering how much he ought to tell them of what he'd found.

A plate of hard cheese, dried apples, and a small round loaf of bread landed in front of him. He glanced up, surprised to see Blanche standing over him with her arms folded.

"We need to speak to you, Captain," she said, sounding as stern as any commanding officer he'd ever heard.

Scarlett came forward, brows drawn down. "While you were gone, we discussed how odd it is that two strangers should come upon us in a single week where almost none have in the years we have lived here. Do you know who is out there, Caspar? Was there someone?"

Blanche's eyes flickered to her sister when she spoke his Christian name, but she said nothing. The deer must've bought him more favor than he'd thought.

"I did find tracks," he admitted, though he was hesitant to frighten them. "But no. I do not know who it could be. No one knows I am here, except for a friend in England who swore to me he would keep the secret of my coming. It could be a trapper or hunter who merely wandered this direction in search of game."

"Or followed you here," Blanche pointed out, her voice soft. She unfolded her arms and paced away from the table, returning with a kettle and mug for an herbal concoction they used in place of tea. "We have never been troubled before."

Scarlett sat down in the chair nearest his and huffed. "It may all come to nothing."

Blanche shook her head. "Regardless, if either of us has a chore outside we must go together or with the captain." The fair-haired sister moved away and set about preparing a plate of food and tea for her sister.

Caspar began his lunch, contemplating the idea that he'd led a stranger to the solitary cottage. It made sense, of course, but why would someone follow the trail of a man and a horse? Idle curiosity usually didn't carry people far from their own paths.

"Caspar?" Scarlett said, bringing his attention back to her. "There is something else we need to tell you, concerning Grandmother." Scarlett held her mug of steaming drink, looking into its depths most seriously.

"I am at your disposal, of course." He leaned toward her, admiring her posture and bearing.

"Grandmother hasn't been well of late. She is sleeping more yet remains tired. She is sixty years old, but until this winter she was the strongest of the three of us." Scarlett's last word hitched and she swallowed.

Concerned, Caspar looked from Scarlett to Blanche, who leaned against the wall with her arms wrapped tightly around herself.

Putting both her hands on the table, as though drawing strength from the sturdy piece of furniture, Scarlett continued, her tone firm. "If something should happen, if she should grow ill, I am not certain she would be strong enough to overcome it."

He hesitated to offer comfort. Had he not promised to be mindful of her feelings? But she was frightened and uncertain. Caspar reached out and covered one of Scarlett's hands with his. "Tell me what you wish me to do. Shall I fetch a doctor? Transport your family to a village?"

Scarlett's brown eyes filled with tears. "In all honesty, I am not certain what it is we could ask of you. She may only need more rest for a time and then go back to herself, but we worry for her."

"What will become of you if something happens to Mrs. Michaelson?" he asked. The beautiful woman didn't answer, but gently squeezed his hand. "Let me think on it. I cannot like the idea of the two of you—" he glanced in Blanche's direction, "—out here alone. But spring is nearly here. Maybe the warmer weather will help your grandmother to recover her strength."

Blanche reached up to wipe away a tear. "I hope so," she whispered. "Thank you for the venison. The broth will help her a great deal, I am certain."

That explains the amount of joy that gift received. They wanted the fresh meat to help strengthen Mrs. Michaelson's constitution.

He realized, when Blanche turned to go to the fire, that he still held Scarlett's hand. She didn't pull it away, though she stared fixedly at the place where they joined.

"In England," he said, his voice lowered, "one or both of us would be wearing gloves."

The slightest smile touched her lips, sending his heart into a race against he-knew-not-what.

"That would be a shame. This is one of the few moments I must confess to being glad I am not in England." She gave him a shy smile, then gently withdrew her hand to take up her utensils. "Please eat, Caspar. After all, I have more chores for you, so you need your strength."

Caspar chuckled and returned to his luncheon, while his mind went over the dual problems presented to him. He had his own oath and honor to look after, searching out the lost treasure box, but what of Scarlett's family? He wouldn't leave Mrs. Michaelson and her granddaughters at the mercy of a stranger. He wouldn't leave Scarlett and Blanche if their grandmother was fading away.

But he couldn't stay in the forests of France forever.

Chapter Twelve

Scarlett woke in the middle of the night, knowing it was too early to be up. For a long moment, she wasn't certain what had awakened her. She held still in her bed, listening to Blanche's even breathing and her grandmother's soft snore. Beyond the cottage walls she could hear the tree branches clacking in the wind.

She rose, her stocking feet landing on the cold ground without a sound. Scarlett went to the doorway and stopped, seeing light coming through the cracks.

Why is Caspar awake? It cannot be nearly time to rise. Though she had no timepiece to confirm the truth of the thought, she hardly needed one anymore. Her body could sense the coming dawn, and the sun's arrival remained hours away yet.

She lifted her shawl from the hook at the bedroom door and went out, wrapping it tightly around her.

Caspar sat at the table, his pack open and several things lying about. His rifle and pistol gleamed in the lamplight, as though they'd been newly cleaned and polished, but he was bent over a small book. The lamplight made his large form appear almost giant-like, stretching his shadows across their little cottage.

Scarlett didn't recognize the book. They only owned five books, as that had been all they'd dared smuggle from their home. The family Bible, of course, a collection of French poetry, *Hamlet*, *Robinson Crusoe*, and a book of recipes which was nearly worthless given how many of the ingredients and kitchen supplies they lacked.

Coming forward with a purposeful shuffle, to alert him to her presence, Scarlett walked around the table to sit opposite him.

Looking up, Caspar offered her a weary smile. "Scarlett. Did I wake you?"

"I'm not certain," she admitted, admiring his deep blue eyes. "Why are you awake, Caspar?" She studied the items on the table. His weapons *had* been cleaned. There was a roll of clothing, a shaving kit, and other sorts of things one would need for a journey. He shifted in his chair, keeping his gaze lowered to the table.

"I have been uneasy, thinking about the man in the woods. And about your grandmother's health." He drummed his fingers on the table, his forehead wrinkled.

"There is little to be done about either of those things." Scarlet sighed and turned her mind to studying the objects on the table. Particularly the book. It had been so long since she'd read something new. "What were you reading?"

Caspar's right hand moved to cover the small volume, resting there a moment before he picked it up and handed it to her. "My notebook."

"Oh." Scarlett withdrew the hand she'd been reaching out to take it. "I have no wish to intrude upon your private thoughts."

He extended it closer to her. "You wouldn't be. By looking, you may be able to help me solve my problem. Then we can go on to talking about yours."

Hesitantly, she raised her hand and accepted the little black book. The leather was soft and smooth, well-worn. She opened it before her and tilted the pages so the light would fall on them. "What is it you wish me to read?"

"Find the last written page."

Following the direction, she came to a page of neat, tidy script that must be his.

Follow the Northeast Road from Larrau, enter the forest at the foot of the mountains. Watch for a game trail after travelling approx. 10 miles. Bearing eastward. Cross the stream into grove of oaks. Twenty paces in, search out old hollow tree. Box inside, covered.

Scarlett's heartbeat increased its pace as she realized what she must be reading. She bit her bottom lip and read over the instructions, then raised her eyes to see him staring intently at her.

"You really are searching for treasure." Somehow, that disappointed her.

"Not really," he said with a shrug. "While I was serving in the king's army, I was given many special missions. I wasn't a spy. I was more like a scout, but the duties often varied."

He seemed to struggle to find the right word, and while English failed him, she could think of a perfect French term.

"*Reconnaissance*," Scarlett whispered. "Surveying. Studying. Something like that?"

Caspar sat back and regarded her with an amused gleam in his eye. "Exactly like that. During the course of one of our missions, we came upon a very small group of French soldiers transporting goods. My men were hungry at the time. We took the risk and captured the Frenchmen. After searching their wagon, we found a strongbox. It looked as though the soldiers had ransacked a wealthy man's home. There were coins, women's jewelry, all of it worth a small fortune. We decided to take the plunder to our encampment and turn it in. But we found something else. A codebook of sorts. That was the more valuable item. I kept it on my person."

He quieted, staring at the flame in the lantern, lost in his memory.

Scarlett allowed herself to study him, admiring the smooth lines of his face, the deep blue eyes, and his black hair. The man's build continued to astound her. He was twice as wide as she was but watching him work she'd seen well enough he was built of muscle. What sort of life had he come from? He talked of English society, of ballrooms and dances.

Was he a gentleman at home? A person of great importance?

He spoke, his words more clipped as though impatient to relay the next part of his tale. "We escorted the French soldiers as prisoners down a road in a forest. It was spring, and everything was wet and dripping. The mud slowed our progress considerably during the day, and I had the feeling the men we had would be missed. I pressed on into the night, when I shouldn't have. We were ambushed."

A small gasp escaped when she parted her lips. "What happened?"

"Two of my men took the box of plunder and ran into the woods with it, as they had been assigned to do if there was trouble. The rest of us fought in the dark. I am still uncertain as to the numbers of the enemy that night. We left the prisoners and broke into the woods, running in all directions. We had a *rendezvous* point pre-planned. That was always how I did things with my men."

"You are a man who thinks ahead. I think that must be wise, especially for a soldier." Scarlett offered him a tentative smile. "And now you are back to search out the box? For what purpose?"

He shifted forward in his seat, folding his arms and leaning onto the table. "You might call me foolish. The man who gave me those directions, Lieutenant Birks, did so with reluctance. He said I had no reason to tramp about in this country anymore." Caspar dropped his chin onto his arms.

"I want to use the money, the fortune in that box, to help some of the villages nearby. After the loss of so much life, the destruction of property belonging to innocent civilians, I want to make some form of restitution. Often the armies, French, British, Spanish, merely took what they wanted. Long marches trampled fields. Young boys were pressed into service. Stealing from the common man happened frequently." His expression turned frustrated. "I dare not use my own funds to help, as men have been accused of treason for less. But using what already belongs to the people will not cause trouble for my family."

His eyes hardened as he spoke, and Scarlett wished she might reach out to him, smooth back his hair from his forehead and ease the worry from him.

"That is a noble thought, Captain Graysmark." She closed the book and slid it across the table to him. "I commend it. You are brave to return. I cannot imagine many Frenchmen are happy to see you."

"Which is why I came alone, without a uniform." He winked at her. "I invited Lieutenant—Mr. Birks. But his father was ill, so he did not feel he could leave the family."

"That is understandable." Scarlett's mind went to her grandmother, asleep in the bedroom. "How can I help you, Caspar?"

He offered her a tired smile. "I thought you might help me search, when the ground starts to thaw. The sooner I find that chest, the sooner I can start to use it to help others, and I can leave France.

And, if you will permit me, I would like to bring your family with me."

Scarlett went cold and hot at the same time. Go with him? It would be something out of her dreams. Every time she was in his presence, her heart warmed more toward him. He was handsome, kind, and thoughtful. His roughened voice somehow soothed her spirits. But to return to England must be impossible.

You don't know what he's offering you, Scarlett. He may just mean to escort you out of the woods.

"Where would you take us?" she asked, trying to sound as though it didn't matter, as though she didn't believe him.

"To England. With me." His voice rich, dark, and warm like the dying embers of a fire, made her heart ache.

"We-we cannot leave France," she said, then bit her lip. How much did she dare tell him? What if he learned the truth and regarded her with disgust? What if he left immediately? She wouldn't blame him, though he'd proven himself a compassionate man.

"Why?" he asked, tilting his head to one side. He slowly extended an arm across the table to her, then uncurled his fingers, offering his hand palm-up. "Scarlett, please tell me. I swear, on my honor, to tell no one."

The temptation to tell all the secrets, secrets she shared with her sister and grandmother, was great. She looked from the offer of his hand into his face, seeing the earnest fire in his eyes and the determined set to his jaw.

"I am afraid you will hate me if I tell you," she whispered.

His features softened at once, his shoulders drooped. "Hate you? Scarlett, I could never feel anything but the sincerest admiration for you." The inflection he put in the final words made them a caress.

Scarlett put her hand in his, and when he closed his fingers around hers, the warmth from his touch made every particle of her sing.

Trusting him quite suddenly became the easiest thing in the world.

"We cannot go to England because of what my father did." She took in a shaky breath and forced herself to stare directly into Caspar's eyes, watching for any sign of disgust in him. "He was a traitor to the English Crown, declared so after he gave some of his wealth to Napoleon. But you must understand," she rushed to say, seeing confusion in Caspar's eyes. "My father was half French. He spent much of his childhood in Versailles with cousins and grandparents. He, like many others, believed in the things Napoleon's government promised, and he wanted his people to have a better life."

Caspar squeezed her fingers gently, the confusion changing to understanding. "He fled to France?"

She shook her head. "He made no secret of his going, and no one stopped him. He sold everything he had in England. He took my mother, grandmother, my sister and me with him. He purchased a *château* in the country, a house in Paris. But as things changed, as the war worsened, Papa thought he must've made a mistake. The house in Paris was taken by one of Napoleon's generals. The house in the country was regularly used as an outpost for officers and soldiers. One day, he grew angry, and he confronted a general—"

Her voice broke and Scarlett lowered her head to the table, pressing her forehead into the wood, wishing she could force back the memories. "They killed him. They said he was an English spy, and they killed him."

Caspar's hand released hers and she sucked in a pained breath. He would walk away, abandon them. As honorable as he was, how could he stomach all that she'd revealed—

His arm came about her shoulders and she lifted her head, her eyes hot with tears of shame. Caspar knelt by her chair, one arm around her, and his free hand held a handkerchief that must've come from his things on the table. He dabbed at her cheeks, his large hands surprisingly capable of a delicate touch.

"I am truly sorry, Scarlett. Did you have to witness it?" he asked, his face near hers, breathing evenly while her body shook with tears.

"No," she whispered. "We were spared that. And then we were told to pack one bag each and be gone." She sniffled and he handed her the handkerchief so she could blow her nose.

"Everything we had was forfeit. Grandmother took us in hand and marched us straight into the forest. It was horrific." She sniffled again. "I was only sixteen. That was four years ago."

Caspar shook his head and took up both her hands in his, even though she held the damp handkerchief. "Scarlett, let me help. I can make it right. I know I can."

And then, because he was so close, and so kind, and her heart fluttered every time he spoke her name, Scarlett leaned forward and placed her lips on his.

She'd wanted to kiss him for some time, but she'd dared not even contemplate such a thing. Here, in the dark hours of night, their secrets shared, her heart would not allow her to wait longer.

His lips were soft and warm against hers, and when he began to kiss her back, she nearly sagged with relief. His hands were cradling her face, cupping her cheeks. Scarlett had never kissed anyone before. Giving her lips to Caspar filled her with a contented joy.

He pulled away, gently, and she nearly followed him for more. But Scarlett came to herself again, aware of the hour, and the shawl slipping from her shoulders.

I am in my nightgown! She pushed her chair back with enough speed and strength to topple it, and blood rushed into her ears as the foolishness of her behavior struck her at last. What must Caspar think of her? No gently bred woman would behave as she had.

Compromising. That was the English word for it. She'd compromised herself. She'd shown she lacked honor and grace. She'd acted wantonly and stupidly.

Scarlett fled, without looking at him, back to the bedroom. She berated herself all the while and did not turn around until she closed the door between them, barely glimpsing his wide eyes and parted lips before darkness enveloped her.

Trembling, near tears, Scarlett went to her bed and slid beneath the blankets.

Blanche rolled over in her sleep, and then the room was still.

What have I done? Scarlett covered her mouth to keep from moaning aloud. *I have ruined everything.*

Chapter Thirteen

Caspar had stolen a kiss once, when he was fourteen, from a girl his own age who practically dared him to do it. She'd walked away from the encounter satisfied while he'd felt utterly ridiculous. The kiss had been no more than a short, impulsive press of his lips to hers, lasting no more than a second at best.

Kissing Scarlett had been infinitely better, perhaps one of the best experiences of his life. What made it all the sweeter was that she had initiated it. He'd certainly thought about it, close as he was, after spending so much time admiring her lovely face, quick wit, and pink lips. But he had buried those thoughts under his sense of duty.

A smile stretched across his face as he finally stood from where he had knelt next to her chair, seeking to offer comfort and receiving a kiss for his efforts. That she fled after sharing in that intimate act with him did not cause immediate worry. Caspar knew the hour was late, and she may well regret the action, but his thoughts bent instead on how he might cause it to occur again.

Her father had been declared a traitor. That sobered him. Englishmen who acted in any way to support France during the war were not tolerated. He'd heard of imprisonments, exiles, and executions befalling men branded as turncoats. But the war had ended, and Scarlett, Blanche, and Mrs. Michaelson were innocent of whatever Mr. Winter had done. He'd paid for his failings with his life, and they continued to carry the burden in their poverty.

It isn't right. Caspar ran his hand through his hair, standing to pace from the table to the fire. It was a short distance of perhaps six or seven steps. *There's hardly enough room to think in this tiny cottage.*

Calling it a cottage might've been too generous, truthfully.

His mind turned to the women who called it home. Somehow, with nothing but what they could carry, they'd built a life for themselves. They'd found a home, they had adapted. The strength of will and character it took truthfully awed him. The more he learned of these women, the more he wished to aid them.

Caspar tidied his things, still deep in thought. He put his packs away in the corner and laid out the blankets he'd been given for sleeping. After turning out the lamp, he laid on his back and stared up into the darkness.

The women could not remain in the forest, of that he was certain. The grandmother's health notwithstanding, they were fortunate no harm had befallen them from wild animals or cruel men. They needed the safety of other people who would care for their welfare. As Englishwomen, they ought not to stay in France. But if they returned to England, they had nothing.

They needed protection. The sort of protection a man of some standing could give them. But the word of a friend, unconnected to them by blood or law, would not be worth as much as the word of a husband.

Husband? Isn't that going too far, Caspar?

He closed his eyes and studied the thought. Husband. He'd never given much thought to marriage before the war, knowing he would be a soldier from a young age. He was second born and the trade of a clergyman held no interest for him.

Then his brother had died just before the surrender of Bonaparte, leaving Caspar the eldest son, the heir to his father. He'd become a titled man.

He hadn't wanted the title. He'd resisted it. His elder brother, Richard, had been a hero to Caspar in boyhood. But Caspar's position as an earl no longer bewildered him. It was finally proving useful.

As an earl, his name and title would protect any woman he took to wife, and that protection would extend to her family. The discomfort of the hard floor beneath him, and the cool air tickling his nose, faded away into thoughts of family. The old house had been too quiet and still when he'd returned home. His elder brother gone, his mother still in mourning. His mother would delight in Mrs. Michaelson's company, and Blanche would be welcome too.

And Scarlett as his wife, beautiful and elegant, would light the whole house with her vivacity.

I'm getting ahead of myself. Scarlett might find the idea of marrying me repulsive. Though her kiss certainly said otherwise.

Caspar shifted, pulling one of the borrowed quilts up higher. Sleeping fully clothed, while necessary, only added to his discomfort. He finally managed a light doze, wherein his dreams were of snow and searching the forest, Scarlett at his side, wearing a gown of red.

He woke to the sounds of people stirring in the area which served as kitchen and dining room. Stretching, and trying not to groan as the bones in his back popped, he rose with some reluctance. His muscles ached, as much from the work he'd done the day before as from making his bed upon the floor.

The remembrance of Scarlett's late-night conversation and kiss brought a measure of cheer. Caspar glanced toward the kitchen, hoping to see her wrapped in her red shawl and going about her work, but Blanche was the one finding ingredients for breakfast.

"Good morning, Captain," she said with a tilt of her head, her hands full of a bowl and spoon.

"Good morning, Miss Blanche." Caspar rolled to his knees. He folded his bedding, stacked it upon the high-backed bench and went to work building the fire back up from the embers. Before long, the room grew more comfortable.

Caspar scrubbed his hands through his hair and went looking for his shaving kit.

"Today is wash day, Captain," Blanche said, causing him to pause. "Would you have anything you would like cleaned?"

"I do." Caspar relaxed. "How may I assist in seeing it done?"

Blanche chuckled and came to the fire with a pot, filled with the makings of porridge if he guessed correctly. "If you have a change of clothes, allow us to press it for you. Then we will need your dirty laundry. The washtub will need to be filled with lots of water. Perhaps you could help Scarlett fetch it?" She hung the pot on a hook that swung into the fire. "Would you like coffee this morning? Or warm milk?"

"Coffee." He pulled a tin out of his bag. "And I am happy to contribute my stores to the household."

Blanche took the tin from him, the tiniest of smiles turning her lips upward. "That is very kind of you. Thank you."

Caspar laid his only change of clothes on the bench and considered the state of what he wore. Wrinkled, soiled, and worn too many days in a row, he wondered if wash day was more for their benefit than his. He didn't imagine he looked or smelled very tidy.

The bedroom door opened, and his eyes came up at once, searching out Scarlett. It was Mrs.

Michaelson, moving with a cane to aid her, and she bobbed her head in greeting. Scarlett came behind her, carrying a blanket. She met his eye briefly, and her cheeks flushed pink.

"Good morning, Mrs. Michaelson," Caspar said when the woman settled in her chair beside the fire. "Miss Winter." Her blush deepened and she avoided his eyes.

"Captain," Mrs. Michaelson said around a cough, accepting Scarlett's help in tucking a blanket around her lap. "I hope you slept well."

Caspar watched Scarlett from the corner of his eye, finding her behavior endearing. "I did, thank you. I understand today is wash day?"

Scarlett was hastily donning her mittens and arranging her ever-present shawl over her head. She put on her boots as well.

"It is, indeed. I suggest you complete your tasks most likely to make you wish for clean clothes now." The grandmother smiled at him and took up the Bible from the basket at her side.

The door opened and closed, Scarlett slipping outside without another word.

Did she mean to avoid him?

"I will be in shortly for breakfast," Caspar promised, going to pull on his boots and taking his fur coat off the hook near the door. He left the cottage and entered the shed. Fortinbras pawed the ground and knickered. It would be wise to give the animal more exercise today.

The deep brown of Scarlett's hair glistened in the early morning light as she kept her head bent near the goat, milking the animal. Duchess gave him a baleful eye and bleated.

Caspar came further into the building, slowly, and made for his horse. He checked the animal's grain and straw, broke the thin film of ice on the bucket of water near the outer wall. He rubbed the animal with his hand, adjusting the blanket. All the while he kept watch on Scarlett, noting she resisted looking up.

"Your grandmother suggests I do the chores this morning that are most likely to dirty my clothing," he said, voice low as if he were talking to his horse rather than the woman behind him, milking the goat. "Where do you think I ought to begin?"

The sound of the milk hitting the pail slowed. "The chicken coop is in need of attention," she said, her voice barely reaching him. "But you have done so much for us already, I cannot think to ask more of you."

He nodded. "I will begin there after breakfast. For now, I think I'd like to exercise Fortinbras."

"Your horse's name is Fortinbras?" Scarlett asked, her voice rising with interest. "From *Hamlet*?"

His shoulders relaxed and he tried to keep the triumph from his expression when he turned to face her fully. "The very same. I noticed your copy of the play. Is it a favorite of the family?"

"Blanche adores it. I have not been particularly fond of the tragedies of Shakespeare." She stood, hauling the pail with her to place it near the door, away from the animals. She wrapped her arms around her middle and came closer, her eyes moving from his to the horse. "I think there is too much of tragedy in my life for me to appreciate all the death scenes." She laid her hand on the horse's nose, standing only a foot away from Caspar.

"I can understand that." He studied her wistful smile an idea struck. "Scarlett, would you like to ride Fortinbras?"

Scarlett's head raised and her cheeks turned pink. "May I? Truly? That would be wonderful. But—" She bit her bottom lip and regarded the horse with longing. "I haven't ridden in years. I'm not certain I possess the confidence to control such a fine animal."

"Then ride with me." He held his breath after extending the invitation, waiting for her response, watching her carefully. He'd contemplated marrying Scarlett through most of the night. Seeing her again that morning, the way she regarded him almost shyly, did nothing to dissuade him from the idea.

"I'm not certain it would be appropriate, Caspar," she said, her mittened hands drawing the shawl about her. "And after last night—"

"I will not kiss you, if that is what you are concerned about." He went about saddling his horse, trying to appear more relaxed than he felt. "Though perhaps it is I who should extract that promise from you."

He saw her glare from the corner of his eye, but then her lips started to tremble and at last her wide smile appeared. "I will make no such promises, Captain Graysmark. And yes. I would enjoy riding with you. But we cannot be gone long. It is nearly breakfast time."

"A quarter of an hour," he said, cinching the saddle in place, no longer suppressing the triumph in his grin. He reached out to take her hand which she gave to him without hesitation. He gently pulled her closer, putting both hands on her waist—his palms fit delightfully well against the gentle curves beneath her layers—and lifted her onto the horse.

Chapter Fourteen

Nothing prepared Scarlett for the delight she felt when Caspar lifted her onto the back of his horse. Despite the layers she wore against the cold, the warmth of his hands seeped through to her skin.

Stop that.

Attempting to take herself in hand, she gripped the horse's mane and leaned down as Caspar led the horse. The door to the shed was low, even the horse had to duck its head to make it through. Once out in the sun, Scarlett sat straight again, focusing on the feeling of the horse's gait. She hadn't ridden since her father's death and their exile into the woods.

"I used to love to ride," she said without thinking.

Caspar lifted his head to watch her. She hurried to add, "Not that I was a very great rider. But I did not realize how much I enjoyed the exercise until it was no longer available to me."

Caspar nodded his understanding, then brought the horse to a stop. She realized he meant to mount and braced herself, uncertain how he would do so without toppling her.

She needn't have worried. Caspar, despite his size, moved with an easy agility. And then, as his arms came around her to take the reins, Scarlett had a great many more important things to worry about.

The kiss, his hands at her waist, had produced similar sensations but neither had lasted long. With his arms on either side of her, brushing the outside of her shoulders and arms, her awareness of his size made her heart flutter. He wore his fur coat today, and she could not resist leaning in to him in an attempt to soak up some of the heat. She had hurried from one chore to another when outside, hoping the exertion would keep her from freezing. But being near Caspar, his body blazing as cozily as a fire, was heavenly.

"I have spent too much time in the saddle," Caspar said, his low voice reverberating through her bones in a pleasant manner. "First the war, and now coming here. When I return home, I think I will leave the exercising to my grooms for a time."

Scarlett bit her lip, hating the thought of him leaving. "I never answered your question last night."

He guided the horse around the clearing at slow pace. "Which question was that?" She felt his breath against her hair.

"Whether or not I might help you with your treasure hunt." After that kiss, she'd forgotten he'd asked her until the morning. "I will help you however I can, Caspar."

"In order to see me leave all the faster?" he asked, his breath teasing her ear.

She shivered, not entirely from the cold, and one of his arms wrapped around her waist in response, easing her closer to him. Scarlett gave in, resting her cheek against the black fur coat.

She couldn't deny the attraction she felt toward him, but she suspected there was more to it than simply finding him handsome. Scarlett was falling in love with Caspar.

"I wish you didn't have to leave at all," she admitted, her heart heavy.

Caspar pulled the horse to a stop and raised his hand to her cheek. He leaned to the side enough to look down at her, his black eyebrows raised. She smiled, though she wasn't certain how she managed it. Life had been simpler before he'd found them.

"Scarlett, when you say things like that, it makes me think you might actually enjoy my company." He tilted his head toward her, a question in his deep blue eyes. "You remember, I promised I wouldn't kiss you? I rather wish I hadn't. You're so lovely, roses in your cheeks, and your eyes warm and grave."

The blush must've deepened, as heat suffused her from head to toe. He wished to kiss her? Scarlett wished he would. If she kissed him again, what would that say about her character?

Of course, it wasn't as though she were surrounded by gossiping servants. No witnesses hid behind the trees.

Scarlett tipped her chin up, studying his lips, and caught him looking at hers. "You are a man of your word, Captain?" she asked, her voice only a whisper between them.

He leaned closer, his eyes half-closed. "Always."

To kiss him, to experience the joy and beauty of a sweetly shared secret, tempted her. But he would leave and take her heart with him if she wasn't careful.

Scarlett steadied herself by taking his arm, then she drew in a deep breath. "Then I suppose we will do without a kiss." With a quick hop and leaning backward, she slid through his arms, down the side of the horse, and onto the snow. She stumbled a step forward but regained her balance quickly.

Brushing the wrinkles from her heavy skirts, Scarlett ignored the part of her heart that cried out in disappointment. Instead, she smiled at her cleverness and turned to look up at Caspar. "I am going in for breakfast. Don't be long, Caspar." She curtsied and spun around to make her way to the front of the cottage.

She heard Caspar mutter behind her, and when she turned to look over her shoulder he was staring after her, a wry smile on his handsome face. She waved in her most dainty manner and congratulated herself on disentangling her heart from his.

Yet when the day came for him to leave, her heart would surely crack in two.

Chapter Fifteen

The women had strung a line before the fire and hung the washing inside, to keep it from freezing out of doors. Caspar, in a chair he'd brought from the table, sat next to Mrs. Michaelson's chair and read to her from the Book of Psalms. He'd performed a similar service for his mother many times as a young man.

After the evening meal was through, Scarlett had walked outside with Blanche to feed the chickens and see to Duchess one more time before bolting their door against the dark night.

Caspar finished a verse when Mrs. Michaelson turned from her study of the fire to face him, and the look on her face halted his reading at once. "I thought I told you to behave yourself around my granddaughters, Captain Graysmark."

His ears grew warm. "You did, Mrs. Michaelson, and I agreed I would."

She raised one eyebrow at him, and he realized Scarlett must've learned the trick from the older woman. "Then why does my Scarlett flit about you like a sparrow unable to land, lest it be eaten by the cat?"

He closed the book in his hands. "I will tell you the truth, Mrs. Michaelson, and you may decide if I've broken my promise to you. Your granddaughter confided what happened to your son-in-law, and why your family cannot return to England." Mrs. Michaelson's scolding look turned to one of surprise. "When our conversation on the subject concluded, your Scarlett thought it a good moment to kiss me. While I will not claim to have been upset by it, I will protest my innocence on the matter."

Mrs. Michaelson huffed and reached up to adjust the scarf she wore on her gray head. "Dear me. That child. She has forever been in and out of mischief since the day she learned to crawl." She glared at him from the corner of her eyes. "She is a very good girl, however, and I hope you will continue to behave as a gentleman."

"I intend to," he said, leaning closer to the woman. "In fact, I would like your blessing to wed Miss Winter."

The old woman's mouth popped open in her surprise. "Indeed?" she asked, taking a deep breath inward. "Because of that kiss, or something more?"

"Because of many things more, Mrs. Michaelson." Caspar returned the Bible to the woman's sewing basket she kept next to her chair, and he carefully considered what he would say next. "Scarlett is full of life and joy, despite her circumstances, and she is kind and beautiful. She has many qualities that give me reason to believe she would be a good wife and a loving mother. Her dedication to you and her sister speaks very highly of her nature. And there is more to it than that."

Mrs. Michaelson folded her hands in her lap and waited, watching him with her light brown eyes.

"I wish to rescue her. I wish to rescue all of you from this place, from poverty and all the danger you face being out here alone. I've not told you everything about myself, and though it sounds proud to say it, I am in a position of enough importance and power that I could bring you back to England. With Scarlett as my wife, you would be under my protection. You would be safe and cared for in my home."

He waited, attempting to maintain an outward calm he did not feel. He'd laid nearly his entire plan before this woman, the one person in the world who could deny or grant his suit.

"Do you love Scarlett?"

He blinked at Mrs. Michaelson and drew in a sharp breath. "Love her?"

"Yes. Do you?" she asked again, her hands in her lap, her demeanor calm and dignified until a cough shook her thin shoulders.

Caspar rose to fetch her a cup of water, then sat back in his chair, considering the question. Did he love Scarlett? He wasn't certain. He felt attracted to her, he admired her. Could those things be the beginnings of love?

Mrs. Michaelson pushed herself to her feet, cup in hand. She lifted her cane from where it leaned against the hearth, then made her way to the dining area. "I think some tea would ease this cough of mine. Would you like some?"

Not particularly caring for their herbal concoction, Caspar declined politely. By the time Mrs. Michaelson had resumed her seat, he had words prepared again.

"Mrs. Michaelson," he said, "I wonder if—"

The door opened to admit the two young women inside before Caspar could voice his thoughts on the subject of love, startling him out of speaking.

Blanche came in with a thoughtful expression upon her face, the tabby cat twining about her ankles to greet her. But his eyes went immediately to Scarlett.

Scarlett, with her dark eyes glowing warm as a fire on a cold winter night, her cheeks rosy, and her hair shining like polished mahogany. The slim fingers of one hand gripped the milk pail while the other held tightly to her worn red shawl.

Caspar hurried to his feet to take the pail from her hands before she made it more than three steps inside. Her eyebrows went up in surprise, but she relinquished the milk to him with murmured thanks. He took the pail to the pitcher and filled it.

"I think it isn't so cold tonight as it was before," Scarlett said to the room as a whole, but when Caspar turned he saw she was staring at him.

"I hope spring arrives soon." Blanche settled on the bench near the fire, the cat leaping into her lap. "I am dreadfully tired of slogging through snow to get anything done."

Caspar retook his chair and Scarlett sat next to her sister.

"I imagine it grows difficult to pass many nights this way. What do you do for entertainment?" he asked, eyes moving from one sister to another. They were so dissimilar in appearance. One fair haired with cautious gray eyes, the other with rich, dark coloring. While they were both lovely, he couldn't help but think Scarlett the more attractive with her strength and confidence, her warmth, seen in every aspect of her character.

"We make up stories," Scarlett answered his question, tilting her head back against the bench. "Or amuse ourselves by acting out *Hamlet*."

"In French or German," Blanche added with a sigh. "Scarlett plays the part of the mad prince with great talent, Captain. You ought to hear her give his speeches."

Caspar grinned at Scarlett. "What would you say to a performance tonight?"

She narrowed her eyes at him. "I say it would be terribly unfair for me to be the center of attention when we have a new member to our party. I am certain you could entertain us with any number of stories, Captain."

"I am not a great storyteller," he said, fending off the suggestion with one hand.

"We are rather starved for something different," Mrs. Michaelson said at his side, laying a hand on his arm. "Won't you tell us about yourself, Captain?" Her eyes twinkled up at him. "Tell us about your family, or your home."

"We will be the most attentive audience," Blanche added.

Scarlett tilted her head to one side, almost coyly. "No matter how dull the telling may be."

He narrowed his eyes at her and stretched his legs out before him. It was difficult to be intimidating when wearing wool socks instead of a sturdy pair of boots.

"Very well. I will tell you about my family. My father passed away some years ago, but my mother is in good health. I had an elder brother but lost him to an illness last spring. We make our home in Somerset most of the year, but we spend some time in London during the Season." He tried not to hesitate long after mentioning the loss of Richard. He didn't think he could take many more sympathetic words when it came to his elder brother, the man who should hold the title when his father passed.

Caspar continued, giving the barest descriptions of their home in such a way that the ladies present wouldn't know whether it was large or small, elegant or shabby. He had no wish to make them think of the differences in his station and theirs. He was no braggart.

Scarlett interrupted his unhelpful descriptions of his mother's rose garden. "When was the last time you went to a ball?" she asked, a note of longing in her voice.

"A ball?" He'd resigned his commission when word of his brother's loss reached him, in the early summer the year before. The family had entered mourning immediately. "I am afraid it's been nearly two years since I last had the pleasure of standing up with a lady, and I wore my regimental then."

A gleam of interest shone in Scarlett's eyes. "Do you dance well, Captain?"

"Do bears usually dance well, Miss Winter?" he countered, shifting his shoulders slightly to remind her of his size.

"I suppose they could, should they move with the confidence you seem to possess," she said, lips quirked to one side.

Blanche turned a disapproving frown to her sister, but Scarlett ignored it.

"And I have heard bears can be trained to dance," the dark-haired woman added, a twinkle in her eye.

"This is true. I saw a bear dance once, with a troupe of performers. He even wore a fine purple jacket." Caspar shifted his storytelling to talk about the performers, who he'd seen as a young boy during a hiring day. The whole event, taking place in the spring, had almost a fair-like quality to it. Farmers and merchants came to sell their wares, young and not-so-young people came from the fields to see about bettering their situations in life, but there was dancing in the square and an air of celebration when so many gathered together at once.

When he finished describing the bear, and the players in bright costumes and face paint, he went on to talk of the fields in the summer and the beauty of the seaside when his family went to walk along the beaches.

The women fell quiet as he went on, describing the countryside, and he lost himself in the subject for a time.

Until Mrs. Michaelson raised a handkerchief to her eyes. Startled, he stopped to watch her dab at tears.

"Mrs. Michaelson, have I said something to upset you?"

She shook her head and a watery laugh escaped her. "Not at all, Captain. I am only tired. If you will excuse me." She rose shakily to her feet and took her cane. "Blanche, would you help me?"

"Yes, Grandmother." Blanche hurried to put an arm around the woman's waist and helped her grandmother make her way to the bedroom.

"Goodnight, Captain," Mrs. Michaelson said. "Thank you for the lovely stories."

Caspar waited, watching with great unease, until the door shut behind Blanche and her grandmother. Then he turned to Scarlett, raising his hands in a helpless gesture. "What did I do?"

Scarlett pulled her legs up onto the bench and tucked them at her side, beneath her skirts. "You reminded her of home. Grandmother is English, through and through. She misses it." Scarlett's next words came out in a whisper, her face turned to the fire. "I do, too."

He studied her profile, the impish tilt to the tip of her nose, her kissable lips, and her long, dark eyelashes. He spoke without thinking.

"Then come back with me."

Chapter Sixteen

I couldn't have heard him correctly. Scarlett didn't immediately look at Caspar. She stared into the fire, studying the colors of the flames. Red, orange, yellow, white, and the way they danced and flickered in the hearth.

"You don't mean that," she said at last. How could he? They would be outcasts in England, and they would have nothing. No connections, no money for lodging or food. And how would they get there? Passage on a ship would be expensive, and difficult for Grandmother to withstand.

"But I do." Caspar moved across the room, coming to take the seat next to her. His wide shoulders blocked the flames from her view as his half-shadowed face turned toward her. "Come as my guests. All three of you can return to England."

The offer made her heart sing and her hands tremble. Did he love her? He hadn't said as much. The way her body warmed, the rhythm of her heartbeat, the joy nearly bursting from her was overwhelming. She looked down at her lap rather than try to meet his eyes, trying to calm herself enough to think.

The sight of her hands sobered her. Her skin was browner than a lady's ought to be, and it was roughened and chapped from working in all manner of weather at all manner of chores. Her hands milked goats, scattered feed for chickens, used a spade and hoe during the spring planting, and picked slimy grubs off cabbage leaves. Her hands made cheeses and pulled weeds from the earth. They never saw the creams and ointments that had once littered her bedroom table.

Her hands wore red wool mittens in constant need of darning, instead of finely embroidered gloves.

Scarlett shook her head, fighting back tears. What had she become?

Caspar's much larger hands appeared before her eyes, enclosing hers in their warmth. Then his fingers twined with hers.

"Please consider it, Scarlett?" he asked, his rumbly voice soft. "Your grandmother's health may improve. Blanche could read more than *Hamlet*. My house has an extensive library." He spoke with lightness, trying to tease a smile from her no doubt. "And I would throw you a ball where you could dance the night away."

His thumb rubbed her knuckles, not seeming to mind how dry they were.

The picture he painted with his soft words appealed to her, but it wasn't real. It couldn't be.

"And what would I wear to these balls? My shawl? And who would come? We are enemies to the Crown—"

"No, Scarlett." He reached up to take her chin in his hand, gently urging her to look at him. "You are a beautiful woman, with a kind and gentle heart. You would be under my protection." What did he mean by that? What could the earnest expression he wore, the intensity of his blue eyes, signify that she did not understand? "And you would be forgiven for your father's trespasses, I am certain."

If only it was that easy.

"Thank you for your kindness, Caspar. But—" She blinked back tears she hadn't realized had gathered in her eyes. "It is impossible."

Caspar shook his head. "It is possible. I promise." Then he lifted one of her chapped, cold hands and pressed a kiss to the back of it.

Scarlett stared at the top of his head, taking in the thick, black curls and wishing she were brave enough to reach out and run her fingers through it. Instead, she took in a deep breath and reclaimed her hands, tucking them securely behind the net of her shawl. "I should join the others."

It would be for the best. If she looked into his summer-sky eyes any longer, she might give in to his request, or kiss him again.

She slipped from the bench and went to the bedroom door. "Good night, Captain," she said, glancing over her shoulder to see him staring after her, longing on his face.

"Good night, Scarlett."

She closed the bedroom door behind her, finding her grandmother in bed sleeping and Blanche reading by candlelight.

Narrowing her eyes, Scarlett approached her sister and whispered, "Why did you leave me out there alone with him?"

Blanche barely glanced up from her book, though she had likely memorized every word of it long before. "To give you a moment alone with him." She turned a page. "I think he's smitten by you, Scarlett."

Scarlett silently threw her hands upward, then went about getting herself dressed for bed. "What difference would it make if he is? Blanche, he's going to leave as soon as he finds what he's looking for, so why encourage him?"

"Because you've never had a beau. Because he's handsome and kind. Because he very well might save you from this place," Blanche added, her voice low in consideration for their sleeping grandmother. She closed her book and then pulled her knees up to her chest. "What if he could take you away, Scarlett?"

Climbing into the shared bed, Scarlett wriggled under the blankets. The ropes holding the straw mattress creaked. They would need tightening soon. And the mattress would need fresh stuffing. The required list of chores to make a comfortable bed multiplied in her mind. How had she ever taken a soft feather mattress for granted?

"I would never leave you, Blanche. Or Grandmother." She pulled the worn quilt up to her chin, noting the dark smudges beneath her sister's eyes.

If anyone deserves a better life, it is Blanche.

Caspar's offer hovered in her mind like a determined bumblebee, buzzing at her, harmless but making its presence felt. He said he could save him all.

Did she trust him enough to let him try?

Chapter Seventeen

Caspar spent the following days working outside, straightening the rickety fence, repairing drafty holes in the walls, and exercising his horse. He tested the ground every day, noting the receding snow with mixed emotions. He needed it gone to finish his mission and return home, but if Scarlett refused to come with him, he'd much rather winter last a few months more.

Every evening Caspar came in for dinner, then he'd read to Mrs. Michaelson while the sisters went out to bed down the animals for the night. Mrs. Michaelson insisted it was her favorite part of the day. She said nothing more to him about a possible future with Scarlett, but Caspar knew she watched their interactions carefully.

Scarlett and Blanche read *Hamlet* aloud, Scarlett playing the gloomy prince with her one raised eyebrow and a scowl so contrived he couldn't help but laugh when she wore it. Blanche had a great talent for accents and had, for reasons known only to herself, given the king a nasally French lilt.

They made Caspar read the parts of the queen and Ophelia, then laughed as he tried to force his voice higher.

Making Scarlett laugh had become something of a favored duty. Her smile lit up the cottage, but her laugh filled his heart.

After nearly a week of treading carefully, avoiding the subjects of lost treasure and England, Caspar didn't expect her to be the one to bring it up again.

He stood with his back to the cottage, staring into the trees. The melted snow fell from half-frozen branches in drops. He heard the crunch of her steps in the wet snow, recognizing the pattern of her walk.

"Give it another day or two," she said, coming to a stop next to him, "and only the deepest snowdrifts will remain."

The top of her head came to his shoulder, and he could see droplets of water glimmering in her dark curls.

"I have seen animal tracks all about the clearing," he told her. "A fair number of them must be stirring again."

Scarlett nodded, her hands at her sides. She bit her bottom lip, facing the trees. At last she said, "We will search for your treasure soon. After you find it, what will you do?"

"I will give it away," he said without hesitation. "There are beggars in every French street, there are orphanages, and widows with small children who cannot work their lands."

She shifted her weight from one foot to the other, pensive. "What would your countrymen do if they found out? If they knew you had a treasure, rightfully intercepted by your king's army, and you gave it away to the enemy?"

Caspar watched the way the skin around her mouth tightened as she spoke. "The treasure was lost to the king and kingdom," Caspar said. "It was never even accounted for in any official record. It belongs to the King of England no more than it belongs to you or me. No one can shame me for doing the right thing."

Though it was something his lieutenant had asked, and worried over, Caspar stood by his convictions. The treasure belonged in France, where it would do the most good.

Scarlett relaxed, even her lips softening. If only he could kiss her again. He'd relived their kiss over and over, and longed for more, but Scarlett had kept a careful distance from him in that regard.

"What would your countrymen say," she continued, her voice dropping lower, "if you brought a traitor's family home with you?"

His breath hitched. "Very little," he said. "I am a man of means. And some influence." Her hand hung so near his, it would be an easy thing to reach out and hold it. She wasn't even wearing her mittens. He raised his hand to touch the back of hers. "They would say even less if you came as more than just my guest, Scarlett."

Working near her, watching her laugh amid her poverty and care for her family with tenderness, had only made her place in his heart more certain with each passing day.

Her hand turned and she caught his fingers with hers. Caspar's heart jumped hopefully.

"We had better find this treasure," she said, her voice not losing its soft quality. "Before we say any more on the subject."

Caspar squeezed her hand gently. "If that is what you want, Scarlett." At last she looked up at him, the pink in her cheeks betraying her pleasure.

"You would really take all of us with you?" she asked.

"Maybe not Duchess and the chickens."

Her mouth dropped open and then she laughed. "I don't suppose taking a French goat to England is entirely necessary." Her dark eyes sparkled and she leaned closer to him, her shoulder brushing his. "But the hens might be useful. How do I know they even have hens in England?"

"You will have to take my word for it."

"The word of a bear?" she asked, that one eyebrow arching daintily.

He looked down at the fur coat he wore and chuckled. Disentangling his fingers from hers, he took off the coat and, in one smooth arc, wrapped it around her shoulders. He came to stand in front of her, admiring the way his coat swallowed her form.

"One bear to another," he said. "We have chickens in England."

Her blush grew rosier as she tugged the front of the coat together. "This is warm. No wonder you like it."

The breeze ruffled the hair that had come loose from the bandeau she wore, and he extended his hand to catch a dancing strand before tucking it carefully back in place. "I care greatly for you, Scarlett."

She tilted her head to the side and gave him a bewitching smile, genuine and unpracticed. "I care for you, too, Caspar." Her gaze fell to his lips, then darted back up.

Caspar stepped closer, his hands finding her wrists, then her elbows through the thick sleeves of the coat.

She leaned toward him and lifted her chin, and he found himself staring at her lips.

"Scarlett," Blanche's voice called from the cottage.

The woman pulled away from him, pressing her lips together as though holding back a smile while he had to bite his tongue to avoid cursing. He'd been so close to another sweet kiss.

"I had better see what Blanche needs." Scarlett took a step back, then another, before sliding his coat from her arms. "Hopefully we may begin our treasure hunt soon." She tossed the heavy fur at him and he barely caught it before it hit the snow. Then she was gone, her shawl flapping behind her as she practically skipped back to the cottage.

Chapter Eighteen

Scarlett kept her eye on Caspar the rest of the day, and the next morning. Though he promised to help them, she had no wish for her good sense—which Blanche insisted Scarlett was often without—to be overpowered by his delicious kisses. She had to keep a level head in order to make the best decisions for her family. Her attraction to the handsome Englishman was not nearly as important as the safety and health of Grandmother and Blanche. The melting snow dripped off the cottage roof from morning until afternoon, when Scarlett finally decided speaking to Caspar without kissing him, or wanting to kiss him, was possible.

She found him at the tree line, studying the ground.

"What are you looking for?" she asked, pulling her boot out of a thawing patch of mud.

"Animal tracks. And something else." Caspar didn't look up at her but crouched down low and pointed to the damp soil. "Do you see these two straight lines in the grass?"

Scarlett peered down but saw nothing, only the yellowed shoots that had been crushed over months of being buried beneath the snow. "I see lots of lines. It's grass."

"But here, look." He reached a hand up and when she accepted it, he pulled her gently down beside him. His hand encasing hers, and her shoulder against his.

The grass was crushed in a small area, slightly wider than her hand, between two straight, parallel lines.

"Oh. I see it." And then her mind at last overcame her response to Caspar's nearness. Something her art instructor taught her, years long past, was a very simple truth. *There are no straight lines in nature.* Trees grew in curves and crooks, animals' paws and hooves were the same. Only people invented straight lines, whether they were lines on a map, the lines of a house, or the print of a boot.

"Is it the same person as before?" she whispered, dread pooling in her stomach.

"The print is a similar size." Caspar shook his head and stood, pulling her up with him. "And whoever it is came closer when he made these tracks. They've filled with water enough that I think it must've been last night."

Scarlett shivered and looked up into the woods, wondering if they were being watched.

"Will you come with me tomorrow, Scarlett?" Caspar asked, stepping in front of her, blocking her view of the trees. She looked up into his bright blue eyes, considering the question. "The sooner we find what I search for, the sooner we can be gone from this place." There was no mistaking the concern in his eyes, the worry in his voice.

Really, what choice did she have?

"Yes. At dawn." She tugged her hand away from him, resisting the desire to ask questions about leaving the cottage, about leaving the forest and France. Could he really protect them? She hoped so, with all her heart.

The next morning, Scarlett woke before the sun to find Blanche already dressed. She'd confessed Caspar's purpose and plan to her grandmother and sister the night previous, while Caspar had been seeing to his horse. Neither of them seemed surprised to learn of his self-appointed mission or her part in assisting him.

"Hurry and dress," Blanche said, shooing her sister from bed. "I need to get something warm in both of you before you leave."

"What will you do," Scarlett asked, pulling her worn gown over her head, "about the stranger in the woods?"

"We will keep the door bolted and the fire poker at hand," Blanche answered without so much as a sniff. "All will be well, Scarlett. And the sooner you come back with the captain's treasure, the sooner we can leave this horrid place."

Scarlett stilled and gave her sister a measuring glance. "You never complain, Blanche."

Blanche propped one fist on her hip. "That's because it does nothing but make all of us feel sour or sorry for ourselves. But here, at last, there is a way out." She opened the bedroom door. "Hurry, now. And don't wake Grandmother."

Blanche had hot gruel, warm goat's milk, and bread on the table when Scarlett came out, dressed in her warmest clothing. Caspar's bowl was half empty already. She followed his example, determined not to keep him waiting.

When the sun peeked over the trees, its golden glow filling their clearing, Scarlett followed Caspar as he led Fortinbras into the forest.

Chapter Nineteen

The half-thawed mud along the forest floor proved challenging for Caspar's boots. When he turned to check on Scarlett's progress, he saw her carefully hopping from one patch of wet leaves to another. "Scarlett," he said, causing her to wobble to a stop. "Come, ride Fortinbras."

"That hardly seems fair." She looked down and executed another careful jump. "But as we are out of the thicker woods, I will ride if you will."

Caspar waited until she'd crossed the few feet to him, nearly skipping from a rock to strip of bark. Without hesitation, he put his hands on her waist and lifted her into the saddle. In another moment he'd swung himself up behind her.

He enjoyed the warmth of her slim figure so near his. She leaned into him, likely appreciating a similar effect.

"Caspar," she said after they'd ridden a short time in silence. "I have been thinking on your proposal."

His heart paused in its comfortable rhythm, only to increase its tempo at double the speed the next instant. "You have?" His voice sounded even raspier than usual. He cleared his throat. "Do you have an answer?"

"Of a kind." She sat sideways, of course, allowing him a good view of her profile and the soft smile upon her lips. "You have offered to help my family, to help me. But before I tell you what I have decided, I must know why you wish to help. And it must be more than you simply being a gentleman."

Caspar considered her carefully, noting the way the early morning sun brought out deep red in her otherwise dark hair. There was a rosiness to her cheeks, whether brought on by her question or the fresh air he couldn't be certain.

"There is more to it than that." He pondered how to put into words all he'd been thinking, almost since the moment he met Scarlett. "I've never given much thought to marriage. I wasn't supposed to be my father's heir. I was to be a soldier, nothing more. But my brother passed away two months before the French surrender."

"What is your title, if I may ask?"

He'd intentionally never told her, because it was easier to be a soldier than a member of the peerage. He'd never wanted to be a lord.

"I am the sixth Earl of Lavington."

The lack of reaction from her eased his mind. He relaxed. "I enjoy your company, Scarlett. I find your honesty, your determination to care for your family, and so much more about you to be admirable. You are stronger in spirit and character than any woman of my acquaintance."

Scarlett's cheeks darkened. "Thank you. But admiration hardly seems like a firm enough ground to offer such kindness."

"For some, it's more than enough." He could think of many marriages that were more like signing treaties between nations than exchanging vows before God. "But there is more, Scarlett, to you and to how I feel for you." She kept her lips pressed together and faced the direction they travelled again, one hand on the horse's neck to keep her balance.

"I am happy to hear that, Captain."

He chuckled. "Perhaps we ought to speak more on the subject when we aren't on the back of a horse."

"How would that aid your discourse, I wonder?" She turned enough to see him from the corner of her eye. "We are in as private a setting as ever we could be. It is quite compromising, in fact."

"Someone once told me that the rules which govern polite society in London have no place in the French wilderness."

She laughed, a wisp of curl escaping when she tilted her head backward. "*Touché*, Caspar."

He bent forward, so his lips were nearly against her ear, and murmured, "My name on your lips is one of my favorite things, I think."

She turned away and quickly changed the subject. "Do you hear that bird? It is one of my favorites. A sort of sparrow, I think." She went on to describe the animal in detail, taking the subject firmly away from where it had drifted. Caspar refrained from doing more than commenting on the wildlife for the next half hour.

Before long, they'd come to the road. Here they dismounted and walked along it, both watching for any sign of a game trail.

"What is your home like, Caspar?" she asked between one of her little hops to avoid the sodden earth. "And tell me the whole of it, not just about your mother's rose gardens."

Caspar, eyes sweeping the leaves and early spring grasses, tried to summon his memory of the estate where he'd grown up. He'd been away so long during the war, and hardly spent much time at home before coming back to France.

"I fear I might make it sound better than it is. It is home, after all. The estate is called Dartwood. The house is large. It's all red brick and marble floors. The ruins of the old abbey are on the grounds. That's where the earls used to live. Back then it was called Dartwood Abbey." He chuckled. "I suppose we aren't very imaginative. But the grounds are beautiful. There is a small wood, of course. It's in

Lincolnshire. There are rolling green hills, farms, sheep."

Scarlett stopped suddenly and pointed to the ground. "A game trail. Well-used, from the looks of things."

She was right. There were deer tracks, rabbit tracks, and no new grass where several creatures had followed a path downhill to the hidden stream.

"Excellent. Up you go, Scarlett." He had no intention of letting her go down the incline. Her footwear was hardly serviceable and worn enough that she would likely slip all the way to the bottom given the mud.

Scarlett made no argument but held her hands to his shoulder to assist when he lifted her.

But he stilled, hands on her waist, looking down into her beautiful brown eyes, gold-rimmed in the sunlight. He wasn't sure how long they stood there, regarding each other in silence, a gentle expression stealing across her face.

Caspar hardly knew he was speaking before the words left him in a quiet, reverential whisper. "I've fallen in love with you, Scarlett."

Her lips parted and her cheeks flushed. "Caspar," she said, her tone matching his.

He bent slowly, giving her every opportunity to turn her head, to pull away, but she lifted her lips to his, her eyes fluttering closed.

He thought he knew what to expect, given their last kiss, but the sensation of her lips against his was wholly new. Her hands went from his shoulders to his head, her fingers tangling in his hair. His wound around her, cradling her against him. The joy of spring infused itself forever in his mind with that kiss, warmth and light filling all the empty places in his heart. Everything he was or hoped to be now belonged to the slip of a woman in his arms.

They parted, his breathing ragged, and he tipped his forehead to rest it against hers.

"I may be rather in love with you, too," Scarlett whispered between her own gulps for air.

"Will you marry me?" he asked, and immediately wished he hadn't. What if she said no? What if she wasn't ready to answer him? A million reasons for her to say no flooded his mind, and then—

"Yes."

Caspar, having nearly forgotten the entire reason he stood in the middle of a French forest, bent and kissed her again.

Chapter Twenty

Though it took a little time, Scarlett finally sat perched on the back of Fortinbras while Caspar led the horse down the incline to the stream. Once across, she watched as he counted his paces into a clearing full of trees. Scarlett slid off the back of the horse and looked about, narrowing her eyes. A treasure hunt sounded well and good in stories but tramping about in the wilderness made it more of a chore. Although she *did* have Caspar for company. That thought made her grin.

"We are looking for a hollowed tree?"

"The height of a man, yes."

She snorted. "I have known men shorter than myself, and then there are giants like you," she teased.

"I am hardly a giant. It isn't my fault you're the size of an elf."

Scarlett chuckled and walked farther into the trees, peering around an especially large oak. "The disparity in our sizes is not an obstacle to wedding, is it?"

"I don't think—"

A man sprung out before her, brandishing a pistol and a dirty-faced grimace. Before Scarlett could cry out, or flee, his free hand had hold of her shoulder in a pinched, bruising grip. "Stand fast, girlie," he snarled, his unkempt white beard bobbing with each word.

"Scarlett!" Caspar came around the tree with speed, and the man holding Scarlett spun her around, pulling her against his body. He was shorter than she and smelled as vile as he looked. She tried not to gag, tried to keep calm. All the time spent in the forest, she had often imagined how to get herself out of difficult circumstances such as escaping aggressive predators. She must do the same now.

Caspar stood frozen, one hand on the firearm at his belt and the other reaching out, palm-forward, in a calming gesture.

"Tomley," he said, voice lowering dangerously. "What are you doing here?"

They know each other?

"Tomley was a sergeant in my company," Caspar said as though he'd read her mind, his eyes never leaving her assailant. "Not a very trustworthy one, either."

The man made a hissing sound that could've been a laugh. "Look who speaks of trust. You came back to get the loot for yerself. Can't call people names when ye're just as greedy as the low-born men."

Caspar, to his credit, didn't flinch or explain himself. "How did you come to hear of this? You weren't one of them men who hid it, and Birks would never tell you where to look."

Tomley wheezed and coughed, spittle hitting Scarlett on the back of her neck. Reflexively, she leaned away, which only made the man cling more tightly to her. "No, but Carrow would, when in his cups. The man has a drinking problem."

Caspar's expression darkened and he took a step back. "Let the woman go, Tomley. She's nothing to do with you."

"Aye, but she's everything to you, ain't she?" Tomley took a step back, dragging Scarlett with him. She kept her eyes on Caspar, her mind spinning possible outcomes to the situation.

"You were the one prowling around the cottage." Caspar's hand at his pistol twitched and his brows pulled further down. He began to resemble a bear again in his fierceness.

"I followed you from the road. Recognized your horse from miles off." The man sniffled, a disgusting wet sound next to Scarlett's ear. It occurred to her he'd likely been living in the woods for weeks, without shelter, waiting to follow Caspar to the hidden treasure.

The horrid man took another step back, bumping her against him when he pulled for her to follow.

Think, Scarlett! She didn't know what sort of move she dared to make. If she pulled away, wouldn't he simply shoot her? Or Caspar? Caspar could do nothing with Tomley, the ugly little man, using her as a shield.

"Where's the gold, Captain?" the man asked with less amusement in his voice. "Tell me, or your pretty little lady dies."

Scarlett narrowed her eyes at Caspar. She had a plan. She allowed her body to momentarily go limp, as though she'd fainted. In his surprise, Tomley's hold on her loosened while he tried to adjust it, his arm moving to catch her around the waist. Before he could recover his grip, Scarlett threw herself into his other arm, knocking the hand holding his weapon into the tree. He screeched terribly as the pistol fell from his hand.

Caspar roared, sounding every bit like a bear, and lunged forward. Scarlett and Tomley hit the ground and she rolled away, just as Caspar landed upon the man.

Scarlett scrambled for the dropped pistol, determined to secure it, and then she turned and stumbled, backward, to her feet.

Caspar held the man to the ground, and the dirty-faced coward sniveled and cried, all his bravado gone. Caspar murmured low, threatening words Scarlett couldn't entirely make out. He stood, holding Tomley by his bearded neck.

"Scarlett, there is rope in my bag. Bring it, please."

She obeyed, hurrying to Fortinbras and rummaging through one of the saddlebags until she found a length of thin cord. She brought it back, still gripping the pistol.

The horrid little man didn't make a fuss as Caspar tied his wrists behind his back, then found an accommodating tree to further secure his prisoner.

Scarlett watched in silence, pulling her shawl more tightly around herself. She glanced away, hearing the birdsong again, and froze when she spotted the starling sitting upon a half-dead tree, a gaping hole in its middle revealing a hollow center.

She glanced at Caspar, who was checking his knots, then went to the tree. She put the pistol on the ground, then stepped up on one of the tree's protruding roots in order to peer inside.

"Caspar?" she called, making out a square in the shadows. "I think I found your treasure."

A moment later she heard the crunch of leaves beneath his boots and she stepped away, intending to give him access to the sight.

Instead, his arms came around her and he pulled her to him in a firm, enveloping embrace. "Scarlett," he said, voice earnest. "You are my treasure, love. If anything had happened to you—"

She returned the embrace, her heart fluttering. "Shh," she soothed. "I am unharmed." They stood that way for several moments, and each second that passed deepened her love for the honorable man who'd come into her life without warning. She loved him fully.

When they parted, she had to remind him about the found treasure by pointing at the tree. He finally looked inside, then reached his long arms in. Scarlett backed away as he heaved, grunted, and finally brought out a chest covered in damp leaves.

Scarlett looked from the chest in Caspar's arms to the man tied to a tree. "How will we make this work?" she asked, allowing only the faintest hint of amusement into her words.

Caspar hefted the chest, testing its weight. "I suspect we will need to be creative." The afternoon sun had already begun its path downward. "But we've done it, Scarlett, and I can take you to home to England."

Chapter Twenty-one

They arrived at the cottage just ahead of darkness, and Scarlett flew to the door to knock and bid Blanche come help them with the prisoner. Caspar chuckled at that, glancing at the filthy, whining man. He'd tied Tomley's rope to Fortinbras, and the chest to the saddle. He and Scarlett walked alongside the horse, necessitating she hop from stone to leaves to keep from sinking into damp patches of earth. He'd hardly been able to keep his eyes from her, the dread of what could've happened nearly crushing him. How had she become so precious to him in such a short time? He didn't know, didn't care. All that mattered was Scarlett's safety.

He secured his horse in the shed, and Tomley to the wood-cutting stump. He could hear the excited voices of the women floating out the open door to the cottage before he carried the chest inside. He put it on their table and turned to where Mrs. Michaelson stood, both girls with their arms around her.

"I understand you wish to marry my Scarlett, Captain. Or should I say, my lord?"

Caspar shrugged, a little sheepishly. "I would prefer Captain, or Caspar, if you please, Mrs. Michaelson. And I would like your blessing."

She pursed her lips, but her old eyes were crinkled at the corners and there was a spark in them as well. "Caspar, then. Yes. You have my blessing."

He let out a breath trapped too long in his chest, then bowed deeply. "I will forever be in your debt, madam."

She chuckled and then nodded to the box. "So that is what brought you to us?"

Caspar glanced back at the chest, then turned to undo its clasps. "Indeed. Would you like to see?"

"I cannot think why we would wish to," Blanche said with a sniff. "It isn't as though it matters to us. You intend to give it to the poor, do you not?"

"I intend to give it to the people it belongs to." Caspar looked into the chest, full of jewelry and coins, precious gems, and stepped back with a wave. "The poor of this country suffered greatly during the war. Just one coin to a family could make all the difference."

Scarlett came forward, eyes curious, and looked inside. Then she gasped. "Blanche. Is that—?"

Blanche peered in almost reluctantly and then covered her mouth with both hands.

Caspar looked from the pale faces of the women into the chest.

Scarlett reached trembling hands inside and he watched her lift a magnificent ruby necklace. The stones dangled from a golden chain, along with a charm in the shape of a W. "This was our mother's necklace."

Mrs. Michaelson, leaning on her cane, came forward. She reached out to touch the necklace with two fingers, her eyes filling with tears. "It was her wedding present from your father." She nearly fell to the bench, reaching inside the chest. She took out a gold pocket watch. "Look—this was his."

Caspar stood in silence as several pieces were taken from the chest, his presence seemingly forgotten, until each woman had a small pile on the table. Several valuable pieces were lovingly identified, exclaimed over, all while he stood behind them. How much of what was in the box rightfully belonged to them? He didn't doubt their claim. He trusted them, he knew them, and the wonder in their voices and expressions were genuine.

Scarlett was the first to come back to the present, raising her eyes to his. "I never thought to see any of this again."

Blanche nodded, turning over the pocket watch. "Captain," she said, her usually stern voice soft and meek. "May I keep my father's watch?"

Caspar stepped back, raising both of his hands. "It is rightfully your property. You must keep it all."

Surprisingly, Mrs. Michaelson shook her head. "No, dear boy. Perhaps a piece for sentiment, but even still. You are right. These things will do much good in the world. And we hardly have need of them."

Scarlett stood, coming to him and taking his hands. "Caspar, we have lived so long without these things, and we have seen what the war has done to France and to families. We have no need of this anymore. You've promised to take care of us, have you not?"

He nodded, his heart lifting. "I have. But, if it rightfully belongs to your family—"

Mrs. Michaelson shook her gray head, and Blanche pressed the pocket watch to her chest.

The older woman took a small ring. "This was my daughter's wedding ring. Scarlett should keep it. But I have no use for the things here. We have patched our clothing, milked our goat, and kept our chickens. Rubies and gems do not hold the appeal they once did long ago."

Caspar gathered Scarlett to him and accepted the ring from her grandmother. "Will it do, Scarlett?" he asked, showing it to her.

She snuggled closer into his arms. "My dear Caspar, it will do perfectly."

Epilogue

Scarlett stood on her toes, bobbing up and down with the waves. Her husband stood on one side, his arm around her waist and his hand extended, pointing to the white cliffs as their ship swept by. "Home," he said.

They'd married in France, after spending weeks distributing the treasure to the poor, to nuns, to an orphanage. The jewels, coins, and valuables were spread to as many people as possible. As were Blanche's chickens, and Duchess the goat found a home with a grateful family. All that remained of their former life was Grandmother's cane and Blanche's orange tabby cat.

"As long as I am with you," Scarlett said, "I am home."

Caspar chuckled and then nodded to the side. She looked down the railing to see Blanche and the former lieutenant, Mr. Birks, who they'd found at the dockyard. He'd come to aid Caspar when he hadn't heard from his former captain for some time.

Of course, the gentleman had taken one look at Blanche and been completely smitten. Blanche's reserved nature hadn't given way to smiles and blushes until halfway through their time in Calais. Caspar had insisted on new clothing for the ladies and spoiled them terribly for a fortnight. Now the couple stood near, her hand upon the rail, and his hand upon hers.

"I think they make a fine couple," Scarlett said softly. Caspar's answer was a kiss brushed against her forehead. Grandmother, claiming the sea air had given strength to her old bones, walked across the deck of the ship on the arm of a seaman, asking him questions about her homeland and listening in delight to all his gossip.

"How swiftly life can change," Scarlett murmured.

Caspar's lips smiled where they touched her forehead. "Indeed, Lady Lavington. I hope they are all pleasant changes from now on."

She leaned into him, a breeze from shore bringing her the longed-for scent of her homeland. She tilted her head back and, in full view of any who wished to see, kissed her husband soundly.

English society's rules had no place on the deck of a French vessel sailing her home, after all.

Author's Note

Happily ever after is my favorite way to end a story. When my friends and I started brain-storming this series, and our entire brand for this new line of stories, we knew we wanted to make it clear our readers could expect satisfying conclusions to our love stories. So *Forever After* was born.

I hope you've enjoyed my story. If so, please leave a review on the site where you love to find your books. This helps others who enjoy romances of this nature to find my books.

If you want to keep in touch, you can find me on Facebook, or sign up for my newsletter on my website at www.authorsallybritton.com.

Thank you for coming on this fairy tale adventure with me!

Titles by Sally Britton
The Branches of Love Series
Martha's Patience, a novella
#1 The Social Tutor
#2 The Gentleman Physician
#3 His Bluestocking Bride
#4 The Earl and His Lady
#5 Miss Devon's Choice
#6 Courting the Vicar's Daughter (Spring 2019)

The Captain and Miss Winter

Sally Britton lives in the desert with her husband, four children, and two black dogs. She started writing her first story on her mother's electric typewriter, when she was fourteen years old. She knew romance was the way for her to go fairly early on. Reading her way through Jane Austen, Louisa May Alcott, and Lucy Maud Montgomery, Sally also determined she wanted to write about the elegant, complex world of centuries past.

Sally graduated from Brigham Young University in 2007 with a bachelor's in English, her emphasis on British literature. She met and married her husband not long after and they've been building their happily ever after since that day.

Vincent Van Gogh is attributed with the quote, "What is done in love is done well." Sally has taken that as her motto, for herself and her characters, writing stories where love is a choice each person must make, and then go forward with hope to obtain their happily ever after.

All of Sally's published works are available on Amazon.com.

Made in the USA
Middletown, DE
24 November 2024